Helen Sabo 00
3

AF830666

x 1
N 37
70
#86 to 94

Ritual pa 95

THE MYTHIC ARTERY

THE MAGIC

OF MUSIC THERAPY

CAROLYN BEREZNAK KENNY, RMT, MTA, M.A.

Ridgeview Publishing Company

Paper Text: ISBN-0-917930-60-6
Cloth Text: ISBN-0-917930-74-6

Second Printing - January 1983
Third Printing - February 1985
Fourth Printing - July 1988
Fifth Printing - September 1989

Published in the United States of America
by Ridgeview Publishing Company
P.O.Box 686
Atascadero, CA 93422

Printed in the United States of America
by Ridgeview Letterpress & Offset Inc.
Independence, OH 44131

CONTENTS

PART II: MYTHICAL MUSICAL RITUAL

PART III: REFLEXIVE SYNTHESIS

Jason Aronson—for a quotation from
page 7 of Strupp, Hans, et al, *Psychotherapy for Better or Worse...An Analysis of Negative Effects*. Copyright©1977 by Jason Aronson. Reprinted by permission of Jason Aronson.

Basic Books—for a quotation from
page 197 of Levi-Strauss, Claude, *Structural Anthropology*, translated by Claire Jacobson and Brooke Schoepf. Copyright©1963 by Basic Books, Inc., Publishers, New York. Reprinted by permission of Basic Books.

The University of Chicago Press—for a quotation from
page 60 of Moerman, Daniel E., "Anthropology of Symbolic Healing", *Current Anthropology*, vol. 20, March, 1979. Copyright © 1979 by The University of Chicago Press. Reprinted by permission of The University of Chicago Press.

Citadel Press—for a quotation from
page 273 of Sandner, Donald, *Navajo Symbols of Healing*. The original source is page 344 of Wyman, "The Religion of the Navajo Indians", in *Ancient Religions*, edited by V. Ferm and published by Citadel Press. Copyright © 1965 by Citadel Press. Reprinted by permission of Citadel Press.

E. P. Dutton—for quotations from
pages 40 and 127 of Bateson, Gregory, *Mind and Nature*. Copyright © by E. P. Dutton. Reprinted by permission of E. P. Dutton.

Harcourt Brace Jovanovich–for a quotation from
page 118 of Eiseley, Loren, *The Star Thrower*. The original source if *The Unexpected Universe* by Loren Eiseley, published by Harcourt Brace Jovanovich. Reprinted by permission of Harcourt Brace Jovanovich.

Harper and Row Publishers–for quotations from
page 3 of Hillman, James, *Re-visioning Psychotherapy*. Copyright © 1976 by Harper and Row. Reprinted by permission of Harper and Row.

and page 3 of Larsen, Stephen, *The Shaman's Doorway*. Copyright ©1976 by Harper and Row. Reprinted by permission of Harper and Row.

and pages 107 and 113 of Sinnott, E. W., "The Creativeness of Life" (as reprinted in *Creativity*) from *Creativity and Its Cultivation*. Copyright © 1959 by Harper and Row. Reprinted by permission of Harper and Row.

Harvard University Press–for a quotation from
page 257 of Hindemith, Paul, *A Composer's World*. Copyright © 1969 by Harvard University Press. Reprinted by permission of Harvard University Press.

Houghton-Mifflin Company–for a quotation from
page 348 of Rogers, Carl, *On Becoming a Person*. Copyright © 1961 by Houghton-Mifflin. Reprinted by permission of Houghton-Mifflin.

The Estate of Terence McLaughlin–for a quotation from
page 87 of McLaughlin, Terence, *Music and Communication*. Reprinted by permission of The Estate of Terence McLaughlin.

Pantheon Books–for a quotation from
page 35 of Illich, Ivan, *Medical Nemesis*. Copyright ©1976 by Pantheon Books. Reprinted by permission of Pantheon Books, a Division of Random House.

Parabola–for quotations from
page 7 of Schimmel, Annemarie, "The Nature of Death", *Parabola*, vol. II, no. 1, 1977. Reprinted by permission of the editors.

and page 22 of Stendl-Rast, David, "Learning to Die", *Parabola*, vol. II. no. 1, 1977. Reprinted by permission of the editors.

Princeton University Press–for a quotation from
page 18 of Whitmont, Edward C., *The Symbolic Quest: Basic Concepts of Analytical Psychology*. Copyright©1969 by the C. G. Jung Foundation for Analytical Psychology. (First Princeton paperback 1978). Reprinted by permission of Princeton University Press.

Random House–for a quotation from
page 23 of Keleman, Stanley, *Living Your Dying*. Copyright© 1974 by Random House. Reprinted by permission of Random House.

Charles Scribner's Sons–for a quotation from
page 130 of Loren Eiseley, *The Night Country*. Copyright© 1971 by Loren Eiseley (New York: Charles Scribner's Sons, 1971). Reprinted with the permission of Charles Scribner's Sons.

Shambhala Publications–for quotations from
pages 288 and 290 of Arguelles, Jose, *The Transformative Vision*. Copyright©1975 by Jose Arguelles. Reprinted by special arrangement with Shambhala Publications, Inc., 1920 13th St., Boulder, CO 80302.

Social Analysis–for a quotation from
page 3 of Kapferer, Bruce, "Ritual Process and the Transformation of Context", *Social Analysis*, Vol. I, Febryart, 1979. Reprinted by permission of the editors.

Samuel Weiser–for quotations from
pages 2, 3 and 97 of Khan, Inayat, *Music*. Copyright©1971 by Samuel Weiser, Inc., York Beach, Maine. Reprinted by permission of Samuel Weiser.

FORWARD

Music is a primary avenue of emotional expression in all societies. In the act of creating music, there can be a truth in feeling that exceeds the spoken word. And there can be a freedom of response in both the giver and the receiver of a musical message that allows music to be an ideal therapeutic tool. Music as therapy has been a part of life since the beginning of recorded history. Music Therapy as a profession is about 30 years old. We are still young enough to be self-conscious, but we are old enough to realize the need for preparing our professional case. I met the author in 1979 at a symposium which was focused on just such preparation. I soon learned that she had long since begun to create and refine her own case for Music Therapy. Her preparation combines a wealth of clinical experience with an academic viewpoint. This book reflects that depth. It also is a reflection of a gentle human being with respect and compassion for all aspects of the human condition. *The Mythic Artery* is a fine addition to the literature revealing and explaining the power of music.

Kay Roskam, RMT, Ph.D.

Director of Music Therapy

California State University
Long Beach

DEDICATION

I thank the patients of Music Therapy sessions who helped me to realize the power and significance of mythic music. Grateful thanks go to my friends and colleagues in Vancouver and across Canada, especially the members of the Canadian Association for Music Therapy, who gave me support and encouragement. I especially appreciate the support of my friends and teachers David Whitaker, Robin Ridington and Bob Poutt, who inspired and helped me to weave my way smoothly through the challenges of interdisciplinary studies at the University of British Columbia. Special thanks also go to the Music Therapy students of Capilano College in Vancouver for their faith, trust and committment and to Charles Eagle, Director of Music Therapy at Southern Methodist University, for his invaluable editorial advice and encouragement.

. . .Michael, who began this journey. . . Nancy, who travelled with me through both dark and light moments of creativity and hard work. . .the cultures which flow through my blood–Cherokee, Russian, Ukrainian, English and Irish. . my parents for the music they gave me. . . my children for keeping the child's mind ever present. . . Dan for his patience and wisdom. . . my spirit guides for light beyond my own strength. . . all of these for love beyond the boundaries of my imagination.

Carolyn Bereznak Kenny

PREFACE

One day I began to wonder about how I accumulated thirteen years of experience in Music Therapy. It was truly wonderful, for as in all things which one enjoys, the time had gone quickly. In the midst of all that wonderful and absorbing subjective appreciation, I was, as we all inevitably are, suddenly engaged in the more serious and objective why's, how's, when's and where's. Why did I choose Music Therapy for a career? Where were the beginnings? What force had motivated me throughout all those years to struggle within the medical community to bring the "healing arts" to people in a state of dramatic need? These questions directed me on a journey. This book is a description of that journey and how it relates to the profession as a whole.

It was easy to remember the "beginnings". I began my career in Music Therapy as a child, when I spent time with the magic of music...when I still remembered a liquid way of being. Music was a liquid form which nurtured and inspired me. It made me aware of the flow of life. There was no question of known or unknown. But there was meaningful stimulation, learning about the qualities of life through musical perception. There was spiritual freedom. As the Chinese say, music captures form and goes beyond form to the supernatural. And there was a unification of myself with all the things around me. There were other benefits which are difficult to describe. However, I remember that these musical encounters magnified my sense of well-being in a magical and trusting way.

Then a quote came back to me from the Bible: ''When I was a child, I thought as a child and acted as a child. Now that I am a man, I have given up the ways of a child.'' Those of us who are parents certainly know what that means. But what innocent wisdom have I also sacrificed by giving up the ways of a child? Then other questions came: What have we, as a civilization, left behind with those primitive, primal, preconscious ways of being from the clear morning of our beginnings? What have we left behind as individuals and as a culture in terms of our original potential for development? And how does music and Music Therapy really fit into this development? With so many questions of what and why, I realized that I was quickly spinning into the whirlpool of mind where one question leads to many, and words lead to more words. I wanted to retain my original subjective absorption of appreciation, the dream-life of the Music Therapist. But I also wanted to follow my insatiable curiosity into that whirlpool of why. For I am in many ways only a product of my culture, a culture which has developed mind to amazing lengths and created an ever-increasing hunger for that mind to be satisfied with intellectual insights and understands—an over-abundant assignment of word symbols. As all nature, mind is a thing of great beauty. We tend to get lost in words. We work to understand and describe the things we love. Music is one of these mysteries which defies description.

For years Music Therapy has been wearing a mask because of our own inadequacy to describe and understand her fully.

We disguise her in medically acceptable terms. We speak only of observable data. We superimpose statistical formulae, hoping that if we develop the scientific side, the artistic, spiritual side will magically emerge. We rarely mention that music goes beyond sign to spirit. We describe and develop the objective, knowing all along that the subjective has as much, if not more, influence on our patients, our clients and ourselves.

This book, in a sense, is paradox. It is an attempt to touch the essence of music in the fullness of all her healing powers, to describe that which cannot be described. This attempt is made in the spirit of appreciation and perhaps as a tribute to the mind of man. Words can never reach far enough into music to touch her essence. However, with the trying, our words will become more musical, our respect and wonder more absorbing, our understanding of music deeper.

My experience when writing about music is entirely different than my experience when hearing or playing music. When music comes to me I sincerely believe that all my attempts at description will be futile, and yet I am totally grateful that this is so. For the reader, if you become lost in this vast forest of words, listen to Eric Satie's "Gymnopedies" or Samuel Barber's "Adagio for Strings" or Ron Carter's "Ballad" or the Gamelan music of Bali. Or, if you are able, sit down at the piano and play Chopin's preludes or etudes. Allow your soul to join the massive mythic artery which carries us to the essence of life and the human spirit, connecting us to all of life, before and after, around and in us, from the first moment of creation through all the transformations beyond time and space. For this is the healing experience of music.

PART I

MUSIC, THERAPY AND MYTH

1 MUSIC THERAPY: Definition and Theory

There are two questions which I am asked most commonly. The first question is: What is your name? The second question is: What is Music Therapy? I can count on answering the first question with great consistency. However, when the second question arises, I always find it difficult to give a satisfactory answer. Part of me wishes that the textbook definition I learned so many years ago could just come automatically out of my mouth and ring true. However, the biggest part of me knows that if I had in fact given that definition, I would not have lasted long as a Music Therapist, for the thrill of doing the work has stemmed from the ever-changing nature of the art. Even though I have studied, practiced, taught, lectured and written about Music Therapy all these years, every time someone asks me the question "What is Music Therapy?" I have to absorb the silence, center myself and think "My God, here it is again. What am I going to say this time?" Every time it is a challenge, a task, an invitation to increase my own understanding by assigning words to something which is indescribable by nature and has the additional aspect of being something different every time it happens. Several times I have been tempted to answer: "Music Therapy is everything and it is nothing," or "It is profound. . . it moves me every time I do it. . . it works. . . it's a flowor. . . it's a waterfall. . ." and the list goes on and on. I find my definition being greatly influenced by the position of the person asking the question, just as much as by my own attitude on that particular day. The lesson here is that Music Therapy is different to different people at different times in different places. Although this is a difficult pill to swallow when developing a rationale for government funding, it is a welcome idea when listening to music and absorbing music, the healer.

What is Music Therapy? The term "Music Therapy" has two parts—"Music" and "Therapy". So let us try to describe each part. We have come to know of therapy as a treatment for some pathological condition. It usually involves a set of goals and objectives, a treatment plan and some anticipated results. Most commonly, it is associated with medical treatment. Our ideas about psychological treatment have branched off from our ideas about physical treatment. In fact, our word "therapy" is derived from the Greek "Therapeia" which means medical treatment. However, as all words which come into general usage, the word therapy has developed broader, colloquial meanings which go beyond the classification of medical treatment. Therapy has come to mean any method of healing which seeks to alleviate suffering, develop potential and encourage rehabilitation. This broader meaning has caused quite a lot of controversy in traditional professional circles. The primary argument takes the form of accusations about people who call themselves therapists. The professionals, that is the doctors, nurses, psychiatrists, professional associations, cry out "You cannot do therapy because you are not medical." The recipients of these accusations call out "You cannot do therapy because you are too medical." These non-medical therapists often represent the movement toward holistic health. It is often difficult to know whether concerns on both sides come from moral or economic values. Of course, it is always hoped that at the base of this controversy there is a genuine concern for suffering humanity. However, it is also true that we have created a huge health business. Sometimes it becomes difficult to separate the means from the end. It is true that we have invented more and more therapies. When I hear terms like "Reality Therapy" and "Hug Therapy," I must say that my reaction is "Have we really gone this far off the deep end that we must call reality a therapy or hugs, therapy? Have we, as a culture, *really* lost our grip on reality so much that we must invent a therapy to help us find it again? And is there anyone who could deny that almost every hug which ever was hugged was therapeutic?"

This leads us to the second meaning of the Greek word "therapeia"–"attendance," which means being present, stretching, giving heed to, looking after, listening to, waiting for, directing attention to and watching over the working of. This second interpretation of therapy not only broadens the possibilities to include more than medical treatment, but it also liberates the quality of treatment from a technological orientation provided us by the medical model. In the medical model, the therapist does something to someone. Attendance implies a mutual interchange, an alert, resourceful, caring, vigilant patience and guidance. It represents an attitude, a way of being. Attention concerns itself with intention.

Just as one might question the term "Reality Therapy" or "Hug Therapy," the term "Music Therapy" might also be questioned. One of the first things I write on the blackboard in teaching Music Therapy students is: "Music". Then I say, "Let's talk about the inherent healing aspects of music." Music can be a natural healer, whether we realize it or not, both preventative and curative. Music is defined as the science or art of incorporating pleasing, expressive or intelligible combinations of vocal or instrumental tunes into a composition having definite structure and continuity. But our interest in music goes far beyond this definition. What are the healing qualities of music which tie it so mysteriously to the essence of the human condition? Learning how to answer this question and identify music in this way is the most difficult and most important task of the Music Therapist and it is the attempt of this book. Some of the healing qualities of music might be:

- music reflects Nature.
- music stimulates the emotions, the intellect, the body.
- forms and structure of music provide a symbolic order.
- music provides a relational context for man in the world.
- music transcends situational conflict.
- music communicates ideas and feelings beyond words.
- music satisfies the need for aesthetic fulfillment.
- music reflects, dramatizes and focuses on positive or negative connections between people and events.
- music is re-assuring.
- music provides a source of regeneration and renewal.
- music is centering or disintegrative.
- music offers high motivational stimulation.
- music fulfills man's creative instinct.
- music represents a pre-verbal or primitive level of communication and therefore broadens the possibilities for communication and eliminates boundaries.
- music is sign and goes beyond sign to spirit.
- music is a place to come together.
- music is a place to be alone.
- music provides an opportunity for release through creation of symbolic form.
- music contains solutions and resolutions which are metaphors of life.
- music contains tensions which are metaphors of life.
- music moves the whole man.
- music is profound.
- music acknowledges suffering and joy.
- music is a resource pool of images.
- music is a reflection of man and contains all his impulse.
- music provides a framework from which to make choices.

- music is a sensual statement.
- music duplicates the pre-natal existence of flow and vibration, always a part of man.
- music is an existential reality, a celebration of the moment, yet transcends time.
- music is magic.
- music is flexible and adaptable.
- music is an alternative.
- music combines art and science.
- music provides a meaningful social context.
- music is a bridge.
- music has an immediate and a delayed influence.
- music is at once process and product.
- music is an intermediary object.
- music is solid and liquid.

Again we can see that music represents change and transformation. It is two things at once. It can and does accept and embrace opposites. Music is never the same. It constantly evolves. This is in fact the most general goal of healing or therapy–change. Rigidity, getting stuck or the inability to deal with a new situation, lack of adaptability, fear of the unknown–these are all the concerns of the disabled and, in fact, the concerns of mankind as a whole. John Grinder and Richard Bandler, in their work of *The Structures of Magic*, consider therapy as situations in which to experiment with alternatives. Such an experimentation with alternatives challenges our powers of creativity. We can envision music as a resource pool of images...

> *Music is a resource pool. It contains many things– images, patterns, mood suggestions, textures, feelings, processes. If selected, created and used with respect and wisdom, the clients will hear what they need to hear in the music, and use the ritual as a supportive context.*

While struggling to define music, it is best to keep in mind the advice of gregory bateson, when he suggests that we develop *relational* definitions. Our attempts to isolate concepts and phenomenon tend to carry us further into cubicles of separation in terms of our general cultural health. The connecting patterns which unite us with all of nature, all of mankind, have healing potential of their own. With a relational definition in mind, perhaps the best way to define music is through images....images which mysteriously speak of our unity. *We are never really alone.*

Of course, everyone will have different images and this is part of the beauty. Music is different for everyone and heals everyone in unique ways. In fact, people heal themselves through music. The attending music therapist serves merely as a resource person and supportive guide.

It is difficult to develop a definition of Music Therapy without considering the therapist who facilitates the therapy. By placing the word "therapy" on the end of music, we are qualifying the term in a way which relates to the therapist, i.e., we are sifting out the things about music which we consider non-therapeutic. The therapist is the person who makes these choices. Specifically, we are assuming that the music we use will be the kind which will attend to the needs of the recipients of Music Therapy. If one were to use the first meaning of therapy, the music used would be music which would function as medical treatment. However, since the "attendance" definition allows a broader meaning and a meaning of slightly different quality, we will consider ourselves musical attendants. This interpretation of a therapist implies that he or she will be a person of good will and good intention. The Music Therapist intends to address the issues of human need, especially growth and change, alleviation of pain and suffering. All forms of art or music do not specifically intend this usage, although some accomplish it without intention. However, Music Therapists intentionally concern themselves with the issues of healing. This means that the Music Therapist spends time developing skills of perception. The Music Therapist must learn to perceive those attributes in music and needs in people which match and set us on the road to health.

With these thoughts in mind, *Music Therapy is a process and a form which combines the healing aspects of music with the issues of human need for the benefit of the individual and hence society. The Music Therapist serves as a resource person and guide, providing musical experiences which direct clients towards health and well-being.*

Now that we have established a general, relational definition, we must establish the place of Music Therapy in the working world of health. Music Therapy is often described as a complementary service. It adds to existing services. Although it often shares common goals and objectives with other therapies, its unique value comes with its more artistic or creative orientations.

2 THERAPY: A Dearth of Creativity

It is often difficult for Music Therapists to find satisfactory working environments. Since Music Therapy is an interdisciplinary field, it does not fit exactly into any other field. It is new, at least in modern clinical settings, and often not completely understood. In one of my first jobs as a Music Therapist, I found myself experiencing many of the frustrations created by this dilemma. Even though I was fairly pleased with the work with patients, I found it difficult to describe the work in medical terms required by a staff of doctors, nurses, and psychologists, and "official" charting.

I felt as though each day were a tightrope walk between myself and the medical staff which comprised my colleagues. I wanted to describe Music Therapy in terms which could be accepted, appreciated and integrated. But as I spoke or wrote the medical language, the words seemed empty, not at all true to what had actually happened. Luckily, there was one psychiatrist who knew the therapeutic value of music and the arts within the hospital. Even though he could not describe the effects, he sensed the balance produced by combining the medical and the mythical.

One day, during a particularly difficult staff meeting in which this language problem was being discussed, I threw up my arms in surrender and said, "O.K., that's it. I give up. What is my role here, what is my job here?

No one has ever told me. You tell me, what am I supposed to be doing?'' There was a long silence. Finally, my friend, the psychiatrist said ''There is no model for you here. You are creating a role all by yourself.'' We then engaged in a lengthy discussion about how Music Therapy stimulated creativity among patients and encouraged them to explore alternatives, as opposed to the more standard role-following or stage-following procedures of other treatments.

One of our greatest enemies in the treatment of disability of any kind is rigidity. A rigid person is unable to adapt to difficult situations. Circumstance may be the loss of an arm, the end of a love affair, memories of abusive parents in childhood, contracting of a deadly disease. A primary objective of any therapist is to encourage and inspire people to accept change, to experiment with alternatives within an atmosphere of support. If therapists provide patients and clients with a cure which is rigid, it is like a bandaid, which comes off with the first shower.

Many of the present systems of therapy, across disability, represent rigid forms of cure and need the balance of the arts. In the standard systems the patients must follow all the rules and often they are not permitted to question the purpose. Depth and understanding are sacrificed for convention. This type of treatment is often justified under the title of acute care. A person must quickly return to a socially acceptable functioning level. The rigid forms are also employed in chronic or long-term care. As long as the patients can learn the language of the system and play the game cleverly they are guaranteed a lifetime of custodial care as a career patient, mental or otherwise.

Creativity can counter rigidity. Although a great deal has been written about creativity in the last two decades, much of it fails to capture the essence of creativity. Researchers who test for creativity often mislead, for they confuse quality and quantity.

There may be a hidden cultural resistance to describing creativity in order to keep mystery, myth and magic in our lives. But this resistance may also be due to the nature of most scientific research and the elusive nature of creativity itself.

Poets were given the task of tending to the emotional rainbow's violet hues: the extremes of laughter, tears, awe and wonder, feelings of beauty and religious cravings. These were all rejected by the behavioral sciences. Contemporary psychology views these violet emotions as step-children, perhaps because they are not always easily observed through concrete physical movement. They are internalized in quietude, reverence, yearning, pain, grief and aesthetic pleasure. Even though these emotions have been ignored by contemporary psychologists they are as real as hunger, fear and rage and are manifested in our everyday life. They are also essential to human life and health.

In so many therapeutic environments experiences encouraging creativity are thought of either as frills or as troublemakers, when in fact they are essential to improving the quality of life. So essential that Carl Rogers has said:

> Unless man can make new and original adaptations to his environment as rapidly as his science can change the environment, our culture will perish. Not only individual maladjustment and group tensions but international annihilation will be the price we pay for a lack of creativity.[1]

There is cause to be concerned about the individual as well. Since creativity is one of the basic instincts of man, it must be satisfied in a constructive way or it will become destructive.

Rogers has five basic criticisms of how the culture

manifests a dearth of creativity:

> 1) In education we tend to turn out conformists, stereotypes, individuals whose education is completed, rather than freely creative and original thinkers;
> 2) In our leisure time activities, passive entertainment and regimented group action are overwhelmingly predominant, whereas creative activities are much less in evidence;
> 3) In the sciences, there is an ample supply of technicians, but the number who can creatively formulate fruitful hypotheses and theories is small indeed;
> 4) In industry, creation is reserved for the few ...whereas for the many, life is devoid of original or creative endeavor;
> 5) In individual and family life the same picture holds true...to be original or different is felt to be dangerous.[2]

Creativity cannot be separated from the processes of life. Mental patients and the ''patients'' in general, who receive therapy, often are not encouraged to acknowledge or develop their creative inclinations, but instead to follow prescribed ways of being. The creative personalities suffer the most. These people are misunderstood and inhibited by therapeutic procedures. An acceptance of the value of creativity must be ever present for these people to develop their creativity towards constructive ends. Throughout history, creative people are seldom recognized for their opinions and products within their lifetime. This is probably due to the fact that creativity, by its nature, implies a type of rebelliousness, a breaking away from the usual way of doing things. Society, in order to preserve the status quo, maintains a resistance to change and will react on defensive cue, considering the "novel" ideas and iconoclastic personality deviant. Because artists are so intimately involved in the creative process, they receive a sizeable portion of the criticism. Ironically, as long as they are considered by society to be bona fide artists, they are permitted to be a bit more unusual than the average man. If one of the assumptions of the therapeutic arts is that Everyman is an Artist, this creates a problem in society's acceptance of the process and results of therapeutic arts sessions as manifested by the personality of the patient/client/artist.

Little doubt exists that in the sphere of psychoanalysis and psychiatry, Sigmund Freud has had considerable influence. His attitude toward artists represents the general assumption that the personality of the artist is deviant and sick.

> The artist is an incipient introvert who is not far from being a neurotic. He is impelled by too powerful instinctive needs. He wants to achieve honour, power, fame and the love of women. But he lacks the means of achieving these satisfactions. So like any other unsatisfied person, he turns away from reality and transfers all his interests, his libido, too, to the elaboration of his imaginary wishes, all of which might easily point the way to neurosis; it is well-known how often artists especially suffer from a partial inhibition of their capacities through neurosis.[3]

Here, Freud implies that the thinking processes and products of artists are results of pathological conditions. Considering the far-reaching influence of Freud, it is not surprising that the arts are not widely accepted as a therapeutic mode. He considered art primarily as a flight from reality instead of a symbolic representation which captures meaning and significance both for the individual and the culture. Of course, art can be used as a flight from reality, just as psychoanalysis can be a flight from reality. The difference is found in the "how", the application. If the individual is encouraged to develop creative drives in a constructive manner, the reality of the world and the realities of the arts can be one in the same.

Many artistic types have been donsidered schizophrenic personalities. Such people seem to create a safe place in which to express themselves by travelling to a separate reality, free from cultural convention, similar to the flight of the shaman. Of course, everyone needs a safe place. The schizophrenic person runs the risk of finding the world meaningless, experiencing isolation and anomie. This danger also can be generalized to include Everyman. Thus the "existential vacuum" becomes a cultural trend.

Although everyone has traces of creativity, the easiest place to identify the personal characteristics necessary for creative inclination is with the creative personality. Once discovered, these characteristics can then be recognized and encouraged in Everyman.

In a study done by Maduro with East Indian folk painters, the highly creative group showed the following characteristics:

1) a particularly rich fantasy life;
2) could tolerate ambiguity;
3) were capable of very complex symbolic identification;
4) had more fluid and permeable outer and

> inner ego boundaries with a strong ego-core, requiring less unconscious defensive manoeuvers.

Maduro also noted that in their works the artists were able to reflect the culture and the environment, while still adding their own unique and 'novel' personality to their work.[4] It is this combination of inner and outer exploration which is necessary if the arts are to be useful in therapy. The artists/patients should be free to comment on the condition or situations of their lives which call for expression through their own perceptions and interpretations.

Some claim that "passion" is the essential element in the creative process. A psychoneurosis may represent a passion thwarted, a good creative work, a passion filled. It is this thwarting of passion which sometimes takes place in the name of medical treatment.

"Self-actualization" is another ingredient of creativity. Engagement in a creative process often depends on a person's capacity to mobilize contradictory but mutually reciprocal qualities. A person must be open to new experiences, no matter how bewildering or unknowable. Creativity, therefore, requires imagination and free association. There are two types of creativity:

1) An accumulation of all information available, then putting the information together into unrecognized relationships;
2) A more common process in which a new idea arises, almost spontaneously in the mind, often seemingly out of nothing and at a time when a person might be thinking of something quite different.

This second type of creativity comes through metaphoric rather than logical classifications. The living human system exercises its ability to integrate and organize a pattern out of formlessness, an achievement which rational thought, being somewhat removed from its primitive source and bound with habit and convention, may be incapable of doing–the striving of the unconscious to create patterns out of formlessness is the same process used by the body so that mind and body share this creative element. Creativity thus becomes an attribute of life. (Sinnott)[5] This perspective does not separate physical and mental processes of creativity but considers them one vital life force.

If an individual has the essential elements of creativity, which could be passion, imagination, a searching for meaning, a desire for self-actualization, a predilection to free association, consideration of creativity as a life force, it only remains to set up the conditions to foster creativity. This is the job of the Music Therapist.

The client/patient should have an environment which allows a person to move freely between control and surrencer, activity and acceptance. A person must have time for both application and reflection, or nourishing and being nourished.

Creativity exists in every individual and awaits only the proper conditions to be released and expressed. There are, in general, three conditions necessary for creativity to emerge:

1) lack of rigidity;
2) an expressive situation and availability of tools for expression;
3) spontaneous playing with patterns, shapes, sounds, colors, ideas, relationships.

Within a therapeutic environment a supportive atmosphere must be provided. In other words, the individual must have total freedom of choice and the right to self-determination.

Creative people are drawn to tensions between opposites, and have a tolerance and ability to work with paradox. This tendency has been described as "janusian thinking". Opposites or antitheses are conceived simultaneously. Taoism with its opposites of Yin and Yang, and Buddhism with Nirvana being the end of the cycle of rebirth, are similar to the concept of janusian thinking of the creative individual. This approach has particular significance here. Paradox is often what brings people into therapeutic environments. Because of lack of insight, understanding or problem-solving ability, they are immobilized by paradox instead of challenged to grow through it. Janusian thinking is often outside or beyond logic.

The relation between the arts and creativity is not mutually exclusive. On the contrary, creativity lives in Everyman, whether in a dormant and yet undiscovered stage or functioning at full capacity.

On the other hand, Music Therapy is no more a science than Physics is an art, as Physics in a sense is no more a science than Music Therapy is an art. The element of creativity signifies an approach or attitude, e.g., Physics is an art and Music Therapy a science.

Artists, probably more than anyone else, have been interested and concerned with the actual process of creativity. It seems that the arts provide "easy access" to creativity. By experiencing the therapeutic arts, patients/clients are able to participate in symbolic healing experiences, and may also apply these newly-practiced processes in creativity to other parts of their life for growth and change.

The 1978 Task Panel for the Use of the Arts in Therapy and the Environment of the President's Commission on Mental Health has stated:

> The arts, if presented in a setting of their own under the supervision and guidance of the creative professional, can provide the necessary opportunity for their inherent healing powers to support the innate strengths and integrity of the patient. If such a healing experience is made possible for the patient, he will carry the knowledge and strengths gained from the creative experience into the life he will take up outside the hospital.[6]

It is unfortunate to make distinctions between science and art, for they can be considered one in the same as a vehicle for discovery. However, in order that the life and potential of the "total man" be appreciated, it is important to have an attitude of constructive criticism. Such criticism is important to make use of other vehicles of discovery which fall under the heading of "the arts", rather than under technology.

To be specific, it may be more useful for the individual and society, for man to utilize the processes, techniques, methods and attitudes of all the arts in more areas, particularly those concerned with healing. Because of a consensus in the medical profession, society has taken on certain fixed attitudes about what can and cannot be considered therapy.

In many cases, the arts could provide an alternative to this condition. Spinoza has said that emotional suffering is no longer suffering when a clear and precise picture is formed. The arts provide powerful ways in which to focus and clarify "pictures", whether in sound, movement, color or shape. This is particularly true in the spectrum of emotions. "The arts can be considered the language of emotion. With their inherent ability to elicit involvement and personal action, the arts may be employed as a counterforce to the widespread passivity in our society, the unwillingness to exercise control and assume personal responsibility."[7] (Task Panel Report)

Within the experiences offered in the therapeutic arts there is not only meaningful expression of emotion, but also an invitation to personal action. The effectiveness of various therapies cannot be separated from the issue of creativity. Creativity is by no means the only path to growth. But it can and often does, constitute far-reaching growth since both the individual and society at large receive the benefits.

The following illustration shows the relationship between important considerations neglected in non-art therapies and creativity.

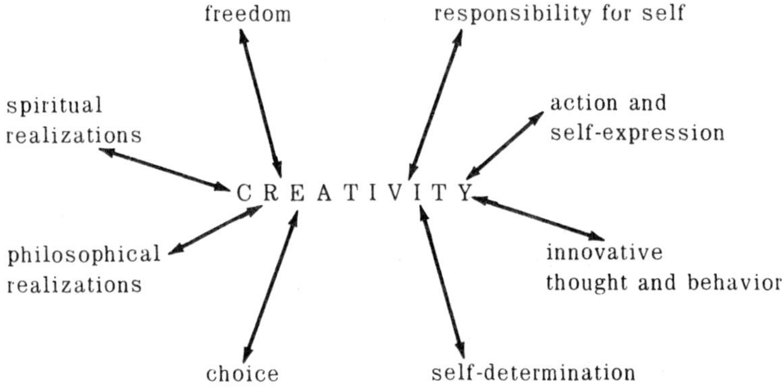

This illustration indicates both an inward and outward movement. All of these qualities or functions or phenomenon feed creativity and in turn are fed by creativity. They are all necessary for creativity, and the successful functioning of creativity builds on each particular category. Likewise, the side categories are gifts which society allows the patient to receive through an attitude of support and a spirit of discovery. The individual represents creativity. If the flow is permitted, both the individual and society benefit from any products of the creative process.

Every element of the model is inherent in experiences with

the arts. Although these processes could naturally be distorted by poor leadership or lack of wisdom and respect, the potential for arts and therapeutic arts experiences to heal are great.

Value placed on the scientific discovery has filtered down into all the levels of our lives. There has been an emphasis on situations, interactions and behavior in general which are observable and quantifiable. By observing these phenomena, data can be obtained and conclusions can be drawn primarily through statistical methods.

Neither the vehicle of the scientific method nor the exact and precise search for conclusions need be criticized. However, the over-emphasis of these means, perhaps even the mususe of them, deserves critical review.

> In his enthusiasm for a new magic, modern man has gone far in assigning to science–his own intellectual invention–a role of omnipotence not inherent in invention itself. Bacon envisioned science as a powerful and enlightened servant–but never the master of man.[8] (Loren Eiseley).

It is clear that science has contributed greatly to the quality of life for modern man. However, it is also becoming clear that it is only one means to search for knowledge. It may be a case of the means distorting the end. If discovery is the aim of science and its resultant technology, science/technology may appear to be the most efficient means to that end. However, what other means are we leaving behind? And more important, how has our striving in the technological age molded our cultural and philosophical values, in this case as pertains to health care services?

Primitive people have always recognized the power of a

symbolic dimension, the setting of boundaries and limits. There have been no sacred limits on the use of tools in our industrial society. Ivan Illich has called this over-extension, licentious technology, which then becomes a moral issue, particularly when applied to the medical community. The medical profession claims freedom from the broad world of law and religion, and is therefore immune to moral criticism by token of its base in science. It does not lay itself open to criticism from society at large but only to its own internal codes.

In many cases, "health" is a one-dimensional concern and does not consider the whole man. Furthermore, people are often deprived of their health because it is literally taken out of their hands. In the case of contemporary psychoanalysis and dynamic psychiatry, professionals obscure and disguise moral and political conflicts as mere personal problems. Thomas Szasz says:

> ...therapeutic interventions have two faces: one is to heal the sick, the other is to control the wicked. Since sickness is often considered to be a form of wickedness and wickedness a form of sickness, contemporary medical practices often consist of complicated combinations of treatment and social control. [9]

Using medicine, and psychiatry in particular, as a form of social control is an attempt to perpetuate the values of society at large and the individual therapist in particular. Inherent in this process as it functions from day to day is the illusion that if a statement or treatment has scientific grounding it is value-free. Value-free cure and care merely does not exist. Unfortunately, many health professionals have a deeper, culturally health-denying effect insofar as they destroy the potential of people to deal with their human weakness, vulnerability and uniqueness in a personal and autonomous way. We unnecessarily become health care consumers.

This leads into the issue of self-determination. The average person, encouraged by the trend to specialization, is overwhelmed by the mystique of medicine and has forfeited rights to his/her own health. Therefore little self-determination exists. The patient is in the hands of the doctor in every respect.

Because treatments are decided through society's value system and the therapist at that moment, the values of the patient and rights to self-determination and self-actualization are greatly inhibited. As long as the patient is willing to conform to the prescribed social code in varying degrees of strictness, he/she will become cured. If the patient has ways of being and speaking which fall outside the prescribed behavior for a particular social code, these strange "behaviors" are considered deviant and therefore symptoms of some illness. The humanistic psychologists are an exception. The influence of the humanistic school is stronger in education than in therapeutic environments. For example, often the only thing "wrong" with the schizophrenic is that he speaks in metaphors unacceptable to his audience, in particular to his psychiatrist. Often what is considered a schizophrenic thought disorder is merely a person's lack of desire or ability to follow the form of Aristotelian logic—the acceptable form of thinking in society today.

It is assumed in these cases that the patient is wrong or sick or wicked. Usually no effort is made to respect the novel thought patterns of a patient, or to interpret these patterns as a sincere effort to communicate knowledge or feeling.The koy to allowing self-determination is respect.

Once an individual has delivered him/herself into the hands of the medical profession, little choice remains. Deterministic explanations of human behavior prevail. *We need to reintroduce freedom, choice, responsibility into the conceptual framework and vocabulary of psychiatry and health care in general.*

> According to the popular image of science everything is, in principle, predictable and controllable; if some event or process is not predictable and controllable in the present state of our knowledge, a little more knowledge and, especially, a little more knowhow, will enable us to predict and control the wild variables. This view is wrong, not merely in detail, but in principle.[10] (Gregory Bateson).

Persons who are ''different'' fall into the category of ''unpredictable persons''. In a general sense, one of the postulates of the behavioristic model, one of the most widely-used forms of therapy, is that human behavior must be predictable or it is deviant. The illusion of predictability currently reigns in medicine and the behavioral sciences. This illusion has affected two particular groups: patients and the general public.

Various schools of psychology, psychiatry and some in psychotherapy have invented hundreds of systems which determine a standard ''functioning level'' or set of behaviors for both normal and ''deviant'' personalities. Even if one is considered ''deviant'', he/she is expected to follow prescribed patterns of being. A great deal of pressure is placed on patients from therapists, family and peers, to comply with these standards of predictability. An individual is rarely encouraged to discover or develop his own unique and perhaps creative problem-solving devices. And the creative is the innovative, the novel, the unusual. Therefore predictability often precludes creativity. This rigidity on the part of therapists is in the interest of perpetuating the medical mystique. Some members of the health care system imply that the individual does not have the resources to aid in his/her own cure because, if left to his/her own devices, a patient/client may encounter an "unpredictable outcome". This illusion is the belief by society as a whole that this will not happen if left under the care of a "professional". The more all-encompassing effect of this illusion on society is the present inclination to forfeit individual rights and support this system socially, economically and intellectually. *As society forfeits its rights via consensus, the individual suffers.*

The over-riding danger for society of the illusion of predictability is that all behaviors, including death, can and should be predictable.

> Of course a treatment or set of therapeutic procedures may work when the theory is wrong; or the theory may be reasonable, but the techniques may be inefficient or ineffective. The point to be made is that the individual practitioner has no sure way of answering these questions since he/she must rely on the clinical method. Furthermore the history of science amply demonstrates that humanity's capacity for self-deceptions may persist for centuries.[11] (Hans Strupp).

Another major influence on the illusion of predictability has been the wide-spread use of statistical methods. The general public and most health care professionals believe: 1) empirical studies prove things; 2) facts cannot be manipulated and distorted if under the protection of empirical evidence and statistical methods. Unfortunately, statistical methods and empirical findings are often misused, whether deliberately, ignorantly, or unconsciously. One rarely finds a study without bias or hidden assumption, whether it's contained in research design, screening of data or choice of statistical method. The area of inferential statistics is particularly hazardous in this regard. Value-free research is a difficult task and seldom if ever achieved.

In the hierarchy of conventional research, studies employing statistical methods carry more value than descriptive methods. The assumption prevails that statistical studies are more objective than descriptive studies. This may or may not be true, depending on, among other considerations:

1) who is doing the study;
2) if they have an axe to grind;
3) if they are aware of their own biases and values;
4) if they are ethical.

The point is that it is easier to mask values in statistics than in descriptions.

In general, statistical methods should be checked and balanced by the following concerns.

First, although some parts of man can be observed and behaviors quantified, there are many parts of man which are difficult to observe but equally important when drawing conclusions about personality types, diagnoses and learning. Emotions, feelings, values, attitudes and philosophies are not easily pinpointed with statistical accuracy, even if they are measured by standardized tests claiming to describe the psyche. Therefore statistical methods sometimes paint a superficial picture of man, ignoring the deeper levels of existence, the unique individuality of personalities which often pertains directly to difficulties in life. Although mathematical procedures can verify quantitatively, the important "shaping" characteristics of man tend to be qualitative. There are few testing devices or quantifying systems of discovery which capture these powerful qualities.

Second, to justify the use of a particular treatment or method, therapists must provide examples of research documenting the effectiveness of their chosen treatment or method. In medicine, it is generally believed that statistically analyzed research rarely lies. Generalization is common through the structures of inferential statistics. In actual fact, the positive effect of a certain method may very well apply only to the population tested in one study. Replication is rare, and not encouraged by publishers of journals.

Third, statistics can be made to show a variety of results. A great deal of integrity must exist in the researcher who uses statistical methods, for his/her research *not* to reflect personal attitudes, bias, values, etc. This is next to impossible but these influences are seldom mentioned in research literature. In addition, there are many statistical methods. If one does not show results, other methods are applied until one is found which perhaps does show the results sought. With the large percentage of research published, researchers have a lot invested in the hope that their particular treatment or theory will work. As a case in point, how often does one see *nonsignificant* statistical results reported in the literature?

This criticism should not be construed to include inquiry, or even particularly scientific inquiry. Unbiased inquiry is essential. The point is that statistical methods appear appropriate only for certain aspects of human personality and behavior. The use of these methods not only far exceeds the appropriate limits, but also has inhibited other types of discovery methods which may be equally valuable and also more appropriate to certain aspects of the human condition. For example case studies would be one example of an alternative.

The fact that the arts are not presently widely used in therapy may be due to the difficulty in quantifying artistic events, experiences and products, except within some standard of achievoment–not always the most important consideration in therapy.

The Task Panel on The Arts in Therapy and the Environment for the President's Commission on Mental Health (1978) states: ". . .the measurement techniques of present statistical methodology are not enough to capture the qualitative and effective gains made through exposure to the arts".[12] Although quantifiable research techniques have been used in the arts, results have not shown consistent significant change. Several factors could influence these reports:

1) Changes, especially internal, inspired by the arts therapies are not easily observed. Artistic experiences often strike a deeper level and change is more gradual and long-term. Often action which occurs from insight does not happen immediately. Rather a healing process is initiated;
2) The spiritual qualities of artistic experiences are vague and mystical, though equally valuable even though they are difficult to quantify;
3) Since present research methods may measure only a portion of the artistic experience, the rest of the experience remains unaccounted.

Studies of the arts in therapy, therefore, are often seen as confusing, giving the feeling of trying to fit a square peg into a round hole.

Sometimes persons are given the choice of whether or not to commit themselves to treatment procedures. Often, in desperation, one turns to medical treatment, including psychiatry. Due to social sanction, these people accept everything which is prescribed with unfailing faith and religious fervor. The psychiatrist, in fact, is the new priest and pastor in the scenario. He is confronted often with human problems diagnosed as neurotic symptoms. All too often the psychiatrist has been trained to employ mechanical systems of treatment and is not concerned with a search for meaning which adapts to changes and touches the depths of soul. The result is a kind of dehumanization of psychiatry. Again, we are faced with the conflict between rigidity and creativity.

Viktor Frankl says the meaning of life changes from man to man, from day to day, from hour to hour. What matters, therefore, is not only the meaning of life in general, but the specific meaning of a person's life at a given moment.[13] Current methods of therapy have little concern with the issue of meaning. Instead, issues of conformity, functioning level, appropriate behavior, take precedent. Levels dealt with in therapy are usually only observable levels. The deeper levels of consciousness and meaning are most often not a consideration. Even the system of psychoanalysis, which has so greatly influenced psychiatric treatment for years, considers primarily psycho-sexual influences and maintains a rigid approach to interpretation of feelings and experience.

Only "things" can be determined by others. Each person is unique and must take responsibility to find meaning and to act. No man and his destiny can be compared with any other destiny. No situation repeats itself for each situation calls for a different response. The situation in which a man finds himself requires him to take responsibility in shaping his own fate. The failure of the health care professional to encourage self-responsibility and action helps to create the career patient. Rites have been mentioned which serve to protect and perpetuate this "professional" monopoly. The strongest influence on keeping the system alive is the patient's own loss of responsibility for self, succumbing to the seduction of the medical mystique. This surrender has allowed the career mental patient to exist.

> Clinical psychology is a remnant of the medical model. It may prove its worth in case after case by dismantling pathological viewpoint. For judging by results belongs to medical empiricism; besides, it assumes what is to

> be established: that the soul's pathologizings are to be dismantled. By raking the soul's sickness fantasy at face value as clinical pathology, the clinical approach creates what it then must treat. It creates clinical patients.[14] (James Hillman)

Clinics, hospitals, mental health centers are filled with people who have given up responsibility for their own health and life. Instead of encouraging these people to take hold of their responsibility, the mental health business provides drug and other treatment regimes which rely totally on clinical methods. Patients come under regular surveillance by therapists. If they do not, they may become dangerous not only because of possible harm to themselves and others, but because, in the patient's ignorance, they may take exception to the prescribed treatment. This strict control is necessary if treatments are to be effective.

> ...the medical monopoly...serves to legitimatize social arrangements into which many people do not fit. It labels the handicapped as unfit and breeds ever new categories of patients. People who are angered, sickened and impaired by their industrial labour and leisure can escape only into a life under medical supervision and are thereby seduced or disqualified from political struggle for a healthier world.[15] (Ivan Illich)

Once a person is admitted to an in-patient ward the enforcement of the value system of the medical treatment staff offers an added humiliation. An even more powerful influence is discrimination by society. The ill effects of lowered self-esteem becomes even more difficult to "cure" than the initial causes of the "illness" which precipitated hospital admission in the first place.

It is therefore apparent that within medical treatments having the largest number of patients, psychiatry included, there is a lack of these important considerations for the whole person:

1. Freedom
2. Choice
3. Self-determination
4. Responsibility
5. Action and self-expression
6. Spiritual realization
7. Philosophical realization
8. Innovative thought and behavior

Creativity can address all of these issues and we can no longer accept its dearth in the field of health care. The therapeutic arts can most dramatically address these concerns.

3 MYTH: Nature, Death, Rebirth

I am the tree.

And in this moment of being tree

I experience both the endless struggle and profound
    beauty of life in the same breath.

We are engaged in a quest for survival and balance.

I hear the music of our dance even through the silence
    of dark hours.

Soon the leaves on my brother will turn

and leave...to replenish the earth again.

I too change.
I sometimes die and am reborn,

As long as we share connecting patterns
    we are One,

Not I, Nor He
    ...but whole and sweet life.

Carolyn Bereznak Kenny, 1979

Because the great body of traditional wisdom is intertwined in complicated systems and rituals, it is a challenge to identify the information which can be acknowledged from tradional structures and described in meaningful modern terms acceptable, in this case, to both the clinician and health care administrator.

This problem might not exist if we had always embraced the wisdom of the past and kept the connecting threads through the evolution of culture and society. Because the pendulum of change can make a sudden and extreme arc throughout history, many valuable ideas and approaches were rejected. Culturally, we are now involved in a rather wide-scale attempt to pick up some pieces and re-integrate many of the ideas of the past.

The Mythic Artery draws information from a variety of disciplines and fields, old and new, in an attempt to make a contribution to a relatively new field, Music Therapy. An attempt is being made to synthesize ideas across disciplines to find the threads which connect our past, our present and our future. Although there are many threads which achieve this connection, music is one of the most powerful because it touches the whole man.

One of the functions of the arts is to remind us of our connections. To a great extent, it tends to be mythic, symbolic and archtypical. The artist has been left to dream and interpret his own dreaming, which has provided him with the freedom of shamanic-like journeys of insight. Music, therefore, is not so much a connector as a vehicle of inspiration which reminds us that we are already connected. And this connected feeling forms the basis of whole health.

Furthermore, this is an exploration into the musical aspects of information from different fields to take the first creative step in the direction of developing useful ideas for the future.

It is a cross-classification and connecting of fields of Music Therapy, Anthropology, Philosophy, Religious Studies, Natural History and Education. It is also dreams, visions, images and spirits.

One of the specific problems in treatment today is that we have lost the historical thread of the arts as healers for every man. Gradually, they are coming back. More and more people are taking up arts and crafts. However, when the arts are applied to therapy, they often are justified and rationalized into distortions of the original benefits of the arts as healers.

In our attempts to become more and more civilized, we have stretched beyond the sacred limits of intellect and are only recently starting the journey back to center. On the one hand, we have the specialized artist, a person removed and excused from the conventions of society at large. The artist is free to dream dreams, see visions, hear voices and sounds of spheres and spirits, as long as he produces art. On the other hand, our clinics and institutions are filled with clients who are dreamers and ritualists and are denied the arts, as frills, because their results are empirically unobservable.

As Jose Arguelles has said:

> What began as the history of art logically must end as the history of man's insanity, for the degree to which art becomes specialized as fine art and dependent for its meaning on art history, is the degree to which man loses his innate wisdom. In recent times this process has been hastened by the machine. Since expression is innate to the human species in denying ourselves our expressive wisdom we have denied ourselves our own humanity.[16]

One of the threads from the past which must be connected to the present and the future is the concept of art as a preventative and curative resource. The most profound and immediate need for this change is felt in the therapeutic environment.

Other areas in which the same principles apply are in formal educational settings and other places where the community comes together to share ritual. There are many general ways in which music can stimulate this change. One specific exemple is the death-rebirth myth as the healing agent in music, which represents the mythical approach to complement already existing medical approaches of music and other therapies. Simply stated the forms and patterns of music can be used as symbolic representations of the on-going process of regeneration and renewal–the death-rebirth myth–for healing in the therapeutic environment. The discovery of this relationship between music, myth and people came about through my work as a Music Therapist.

I have noticed that patients often produce poems, movements, paintings, verbal descriptions and musical improvisations with the death-rebirth myth, or some situation which strongly suggests the death-rebirth myth. These results have come without any suggestion on my part. As guide in those sessions, I became curious about the influences on my own choice of music and instructions to patients which may have been leading to death-rebirth themes.

I have discovered two main influences directing the death-rebirth response:

1) Directions often encouraged patients to develop images of death-rebirth processes in Nature.
2) Music always had an obvious tension/resolution element.

Pinpointing these two influences has encouraged me to examine them in greater depth. This approach was not conceptualized and then applied. Rather, it has emerged from patients and clients themselves, then formulated into the present description.

Before developing an approach which would make use of

the healthy functions of myth, we must clear up some misconceptions about the term itself. The most simplified definition of myth is that it is a widespread cultural story. There is usually a message in the myth beyond the story, a helpful hint about how to live. Because we experience myth through rituals and rituals are associated with "magic", modern man finds it difficult to accept the concept of myth. Myth has been distorted in general usage to mean an untrue story, something which only seems true.

Because of the scientific orientation of our cultural attitudes, ideas about the nature of the universe which cannot be verified by experiment are considered myth. This is how we find ourselves in relation to myth at the present time. But we are coming into a time of myth once again.

> Against the background of history, the eye-opening years of our rational, scientific enlightenment seem a brief moment in the morning of consciousness. We have culturally yawned and stretched a little, but the shadow, the myth-susceptible dreamer is still there just below the surface of our new-found awareness.[17] (Stephen Larsen).

Myth can be considered a synthetic mode of experience which travels through our holistic awareness. It connects us and relates us to our surrounding world through perception, which is not always empirically testable. It comes to us through patterns and archetypes which affect external life indirectly through symbolic activity (Dimmitt-Church). Thus through myth we are able to externalize our individual human hopes and fears into the cultural context and experience them as "shared" phenomena.

The same is true of music. Musical experience is also difficult to test and the benefits equally difficult to perceive. Music also allows us to externalize our human feelings, by expressing and sharing them.

Regarding the function of myth, Joseph Campbell expresses one of the functions to be a shift of emphasis from the individual to the group. Myth is a wonder which man cannot easily explain, an informing energy, a reminder that the whole world is Divine. For the Navaho people, myths affirm that there is rhyme and reason in a world full of hazards.

If we always deal with the difficulties of life in isolation, as the individual, and never relate ourselves to the whole, any solution or cure is likely to be merely an illusion, and short-lived. Many of the modern systems of therapy concentrate entirely on the individual. The individual is brought into group therapy only after there is a coming to grips with "self". Even some of the group therapies are ego-centered and deal primarily with each person's individual needs as opposed to the concerns of the group as a whole. The priority of "I" is obvious, even in many therapeutic communities. As long as group members are making music, working in the garden or cooking together, a community spirit prevails. But the moment verbal psychotherapeutic groups begin, the shift is back to the "I".

There is an intimate relationship between myth and ritual. Ritual is the form through which we experience myth. The beauty of myth is that it takes what "facts" it has and molds, shapes and utilizes these "knowns" through an intuitive, emotional expression. One difference between the myth-makers of old and modern myth-makers is in the interpretation of the meaning of "facts". As a culture, we generally believe that we cannot know something to be a fact unless it has been empirically proven. However, the ancients knew many things which they had not observed in the form of hard data. They knew things which they heard in dreams, the stories of their grandfathers, the coming of events. Myth was a reality and ritual, a response an affirmation of that reality. In other words, we go with what we have, searching for the bare bones of mythic content left for us, the common territory which unites people, and also begin to create rituals in which to relive myth.

One of the results of myth and ritual is symbolic healing. If we, in fact, are able to listen to the mythic messages coming through the symbol codes contained in ritual, they have the power to change our lives. The symbols contained in ritual are many and complex. Music is a symbol of myth representing the past. It is also a symbol of every person present as well as the whole community. In addition to being all of these things in a symbolic sense, it delivers the message, which evolves through the ritual time. It is also unique each time it is performed or perceived, influenced by the beliefs, character, and situation of the group and its members.

Symbolic healing is integral to the use of the myth. Within symbolic healing, the symbol, in this case the music embodying the death-rebirth myth, has some spiritual, psychological, physical effect and inspires a healing of some damaged part of personality. In this case, by stimulating the person to identify with the process of death-rebirth,the person is able to experience a metaphoric dying and rebirth. Metaphoric dying engages the psyche on some level, whether through cognitive recognition or spiritual inspiration. This reaction is difficult to monitor from behavior and may take the form of learning from corrective experience, acquiring new insight, identifying the similarities between symbolic death-rebirth and some present life dilemma.

Since there are many interpretations of what constitutes "symbol", it is important to clarify its meaning here. Whitmont, in *The Symbolic Quest,* defines symbol as "the expression of a spontantous experience which points beyond itself to a meaning not conveyed by a rational term, owing to the latter's intrinsic limitation.''[18]

Some consider symbolism to be a revelation of reality, a message that speaks of passage from one world of meaning to another, sometimes Divine to human or vice versa. For present purposes, all of these ideas shed some understanding on "symbol''. But Suzanne Langer's (1953) simplified definition will serve both to clarify the meaning and to establish an important link which will be discussed later: Symbol is anything which may function as the vehicle for a conception. In this case the music is the vehicle which establishes a relation between the mythic concept of death-rebirth and the people participating in the musical experience.

For the Navaho, symbols not only provide a vocabulary and an explanation but also change the psyche by converting energy into a different form, a form that can heal. A "sing'' means a healing ceremony to the Navaho people. Describing a healing ceremony of the Cuna Indians of Panama, Levi-Strauss says:

> Once the sick woman understands, she does more than resign herself, she gets well. But no such thing happens to our sick when the causes of their diseases have been explained to them in terms of secretions, germs or viruses. We shall perhaps be accused of paradox if we answer that the reason lies in the fact that microbes exist and monsters do not. And yet, the relationship between germ and disease is external to the mind of the patient, for it is a cause and effect relationship; whereas the relationship between monster and disease in internal to his mind, whether conscious or unconscious; it is a relationship between symbol and thing symbolized, or between sign and meaning. The shaman provides the sick woman with a language, by means of which unexpressed, and otherwise inexpressible, psychic states can be immediately expressed.[19]

Symbols bring the patient to his inner resources. If the healing images are strong enough, if the medicine man is skillful and unwavering in his purpose, and if the patient's involvement is deep and urgent, then healing can be expected to occur. The same process can be applied to current "therapies". This brings up the question of specific disabilities. In light of present medical knowledge, these nature cures could be read as dealing with psychological or spiritual "lack of resources" only. However, enough research has accumulated to safely conclude that the mind-body separation theory is on the wane. These areas of research include biofeedback, altered states of consciousness and neurophysiology. It is becoming clear that mind and body are part of the same whole and thus are mutually affected by stimulus. The category of illness pertaining to this information is the area of psychosomatic "diseases". There is a relationship between symbol and substance, mind and body, psychological/sociological phenomena and physical symptoms, mental acts and physical life. Studies in neuro-physiology have identified one of the links between mind and body in the center of the autonomic nervous system, the hypothalmus.

> ...the power of the metaphor, a 'strategic prediction' can move us, that is, change our minds and lead us to behavior change. Metaphorical structure, the system of meaning of a healing discipline is decisive in its effectiveness as much as drugs...as in Native healing rituals where both drugs and songs and dances are felt to have equal impact.[20] (Moerman)

Since symbolic healing occurs both in and between mind and body, the metaphoric and the physiological, it represents a holistic approach. The relation between symbolic healing and tho death-rebirth myth is that the whole person experiences or learns about the value of the death-rebirth process, on its various levels from actual death to some temporary situational loss. The four basic forms or archetypical principles of symbolic healing in Navaho rituals are:

1) a return to the origin or source, the Creation of the world;
2) management of "evil";
3) the restoration of a stable universe;
4) the theme of death-rebirth.

But symbol is more than all of this, for it is meaning. It is reality which points to the ultimate realities of life-death. It is release from suffering and a source of strength.

The Regenerative Experience

Within religious and cultural systems, the regenerative experience has always been valued as one of man's basic healers. In some, as will be illustrated, the cycle of regeneration provides the reason for being, the essence of meaning to life.

Buddhism is based on the continuous cycle of death and rebirth. One never really dies. One is born again many times until the achievement of Nirvana. This process may take a person through many bodies and many ages. Each life is related to the past lives and each life strives to complete the unfinished business of the past (karma).

Within the Zen system, dead and alive are not opposite conditions. According to the principles of Buddhism, nothing ever really ends.Things and people are simply in a constant flow of change.

In the Hindu tradition, the *Bhagavad Gita* tells us that death is certain for the born, and birth is certain for the dead.

The poet Maulana Jalaluddin Rumi, the most influential figure in the development of Islamic thought, says that:

> All follows the rule that sacrifice is necessary to reach a higher goal. The field must be ploughed, in order to receive the seed; the seed grows and is harvested and the grains are crushed under the millstone; the flour, then, has to endure the process of baking in order to become bread, which will be crushed again by man's teeth. But by this constant succession of sacrifices the grain will finally become part and parcel of the human nature and will thus participate to a certain extent in the human soul and spirit.[21]

Another Eastern philosopher, Gurdjieff, says:

> Attachment to things keeps alive a thousand useless I's in a man. These I's must die in order that the big I may be born. Continual consciousness of his nothingness and of his helplessness will eventually give a man the courage to "die", that is, to die, not merely mentally or in theory, but to die in fact and to renounce actually and forever those aspects of himself which are either unnecessary to the point of view of his inner growth, or which hinder it.[22]

Christian philosophy and practice is based on the model of Christ, who died, only to be born again, transcending life on earth, achieving a higher state of existence. The baptism ritual allows a person to become born again by dying to original sin.

Brother David Steindl-Rast, a Benedictine Monk, provides a useful interpretation of the Christian approach to death, focusing on the similarities between Eastern and Western thought. He says that one of the basic approaches to daily life in the monastery is to have death at all times before one's eyes. "It is seeing of every life against the horizon of death,and a challenge to incorporate that awareness of dying into every moment so as to become more fully alive."[23] He makes a distinction between purpose and meaning. We live by meaning and often lose the meaning by getting lost in purpose. This Christian interpretation echoes the non.-attachment principles we hear so often with the Zen tradition.

In the end, we have only what we give up. For things live only in the flow of *all* things. In the relationship between mother and child, a child is "let go" many times by the mother, through the stages of development. This is a type of dying over and over again.

In the Navaho culture, death and rebirth are the mythological symbols for a psychological event. Like the sun, the ego must prepare itself for a plunge into the darkness of the unconscious world, there to experience rejuvenation. The symbolic process of death and rebirth is found wherever there is a life crisis necessitating rites of transformation rechanneling psychic energy from old patterns to more functional new ones.

Here we can identify the relevance of the death-rebirth myth for man today. The application would be the same. Not only does the myth have great meaning for each person in individual life, but it also serves the other important group function through identifying what Joseph Campbell calls an elementary idea, that is, an idea which applies to all people, a human constant. This second function adds depth and meaning and encourages people to consider themselves in relation to other beings. One person is not alone in suffering, for suffering is an integral part of human life. If suffering is to be endured, it must have meaning.

The death-rebirth myth, if accepted and experienced through cultural ritual of some kind, can be "meaningful".

Death and rebirth connect the psyche to the on-going processes and rhythms of life. Any one of life's situations can provide a context for this universal myth. Victor Frankl speaks of life in the concentration camp. He says that, to survive and find some meaning for existence, the prisoners went through a phase of apathy or what he calls "emotional death". Once they had "died" and reduced their psyche to the most basic level of existence, they were prepared to be reborn again in the concentration camp. Frankl suggests that people do not need a tensionless state, but instead require a striving and struggling for some worthy goal.

The Salish Guardian Spirit Dance Ceremonies, like many Native rituals, provide an example of how the regenerative experience is used as a healer with a social/spiritual system. The initiates, who are usually young people having some problem in life, are encouraged to die to the white man's ways and be reborn again as a true Indian. Through the rituals of Guardian Spirit Ceremonials, participants sing, dance, fast, costume, train and undergo a type of symbolic death which frees them from both corrupt influences, such as drugs and alcohol, and anomie resulting from a lack of cultural identity. Once a person has been initiated in these ceremonials, he or she is eligible to dance every season in order to renew personal healing. Guardian Spirit Dances are rituals which have been reinstated into the Longhouse by the Salish people to add healing for members of the band today.

Rituals of initiation, transformation, creation, the hero myths, all relate to death-rebirth. Each re-enacted situation implies going through some difficult experience, dying to part of self or letting go of something or someone and being transformed, reborn, or greatly changed in some way.

Initiation lies at the core of any genuine human life. And this is true for two reasons. First, any genuine human life implies profound crises, ordeals, suffering, loss and reconquest of self, "death and resurrection". Second, whatever degrees of fulfillment it may have brought him at a certain moment, every man sees his life as a failure. The hope and dream of these moments of total crisis are to obtain a definitive and total "renovation", a renewal capable of transmuting life.[24] (Eliade).

Since the medical community functions primarily as a closed body or society, its own internal systems are considered more relevant than the ways of the past–certain esoteric psychologies or religious philosophies. These resources are rarely integrated into the scientific body of knowledge. The regenerative or transformative experience as described here is not employed on a conscious level. Certainly the full potential of the death-rebirth myth as a healer has not as yet been explored in therapeutic settings. However, in the past five years, the topics of actual death and symbolic death have received attention on a theoretical and in some cases practical level. This change hopefully represents a catalyst which in the near future will produce a direct result in the world of "therapies". The basic message of this literature is to consider the act of physical death-rebirth as one step in many "dying" steps in life. The assumption is that death is one of the inevitable laws of nature. Instead of thinking about death with fear and denial, it is possible to consider it as part of the on-going process of life. Without death, there is no life, without life, there is no death. An attitude about death reflects an attitude about life. It is hoped that if one comes to accept the inevitability, necessity and even value of death, the same insight will apply to life and particular life situations.

> Discovering our dying is a turning point. Dying evokes the helplessness, the unexpected, challenging the unknown. Dying establishes new directions, gaining new powers, loosing the old; Giving up action patterns, thought patterns, being unsure, being excited, knowing something is emerging but not knowing where it is going. Dying, like any turning point, is a place of transition, a facing of the unknown and the emerging complexity of new ways of being, new actions, thoughts, feelings. Each turning point is the realization of loss, an encounter with the unknown.[25] (Stanley Keleman)

The connection between physical death and symbolic death, physical rebirth and symbolic rebirth represents a level of acceptance and understanding which allows for the nurturing of insight about concrete situations in life.

Nature as Teacher and Healer

> The human brain, so frail, so perishable, so full of inexhaustible dreams and hungers, burns by the power of the leaf. A few moments loss of vital air and the phenomenon we know as consciousness goes down into the black night of inorganic things. The human body is a magical vessel, but its life is linked with an element it cannot produce. Only the green plant knows the secret of transforming the light that comes to us across the far reaches of space. There is no better illustration of the intimacy of man's relationship with other living things.[26] (Loren Eiseley)

Eiseley speaks of the "secret of transforming". The

process of regeneration is evident at every turning as man confronts his environment–the process of birth, maturity, decay, rebirth. Physical elements never die, but are always recycled into another form. This process is visible in a forest, a tidal pool and in man's own creations. In a sense these situations are metaphors of man's own life. Both must learn how to survive by giving in to the process of life and death. Survival for a great percentage of the natural world is a matter of instinct. Every Winter leaves will fall, decay and nourish new growth for Spring. Bears will hibernate. Salmon will spawn. However, because of the nature of human intelligence, this survival instinct is not always so clear in the human. Men and women can manipulate their environment and often do so without considering the consequences in terms of survival. Therapy can be considered as a type of training in survival skills for the human being. Nature allows people to learn about survival. But Nature does not simply represent reality. In the shapes of life, Nature prepares the future; it offers alternatives. Another value of accepting Nature as teacher, is that by appreciating our connections to the Earth and fellow living creatures, we are able to shed our feeling of alienation. One can recognize that he or she is part of a framework (of Nature) and that the same processes, in fact creative processes, going on around a person are also going on in oneself. People realize that they are connected to their environment, not alone, and in fact are part of a whole, shared existence of Life. Native Indian cultures actively acknowledge this vital link and the significance of appreciating the link for survival.

> There is no quiet place in the white man's cities, no place to hear the leaves of Spring or the rustle of insects' wings. And what is there to life if a

> man cannot hear the lovely cry of a whippoorwill or the arguments of the frogs around a pond at night? The Indian prefers the soft sound of the wind darting over the face of the pond, and the smell of the wind itself cleansed by a mid-day rain, or scented with a pinon pine. The air is precious to the redman. For all things share the same breath–the beasts, the trees, the man. The white man does not seem to notice the air he breathes. Like a man dying for many days, he is numb to the stench.
>
> What is man without the beasts? If all the beasts were gone, men would die from great loneliness of spirit, for whatever happens to the beast also happens to man. All things are *connected.* Whatever befalls the earth befalls the sons of earch.[27] (Chief Sealth)

The Indian considered Nature, and man as part of Nature, Divine and Sacred. Chief Sealth's comments that "all things are connected" points to essential needs in our psychological and physical well-being. He implies that in order to survive people must appreciate the link between themselves and the natural world. The power of Nature is awesome. We have only to witness a storm at sea to know it. Instead of striving to conquer, master, manipulate this power, we can work with it to receive aid in resolving inner conflicts.

The Native peoples accomplish this through symbolic identification and unfailing respect. Nature is not only that which can be observed, but a vital force which somehow manages to keep the elements in balance and harmony and must therefore have wisdom far beyond our knowledge.

The Navaho religion provides the ritual for healing through a profound meditation on nature and its curative powers. In fact, healing is the main focus of all religious activity. And healing is not directed toward specific symptoms or bodily organs, but toward bringing the psyche into harmony with the whole gamut of natural and supernatural forces around it. The medicine of the white man has often failed when competing with this "Indian medicine" which encourages relational well-being.

The themes of Nature as teacher and healer are themes of water, air, forest, wind, growth. When the death-rebirth myth is used in healing, it is rarely identified as the "death-rebirth myth". Instead, it is contained in the images of Nature suggested by the therapist or participants themselves. This encourages the unity which is accomplished in the Navaho "sings" and other ceremonials.

> Religion revolves around a great open secret which we all know but want to hear again and again. In this regard Navaho dogma connects all things, natural and experienced, from man's skeleton to universal destiny, which encompasses even inconceivable space, in a closely interlocking unity which omits nothing, no matter how small or stupendous, and in which each individual has a significant function until, at his final dissolution, he not only becomes one with the ultimate harmony, but he is that harmony.[28] (Sandner)

Patterns

Two key concepts which emerge from the above discussions of myth, death and rebirth and Nature are connections and patterns. These two concepts are not often heard in therapeutic models initiated by the medical community. However, they represent key concepts in the on-going healing, whether preventative or curative, of Native cultures.

"Patterning" is an aesthetic process. We usually think of patterns as the business of artists. Artists see connecting patterns which we do not see. Composers hear connecting patterns which we do not hear. We have learned that perception is largely a matter of selection. In order for us to survive sensory overload, we select only those things which our senses absolutely need. We cannot possibly see and hear and feel and smell and taste all the things which exist or we would drown in sensory stimulation. However, we do train ourselves, according to our priorities, to accept some things and reject others. Unfortunately, both educational and therapeutic environments neglect the development of the artist in everyone. Connecting patterns break the barriers of linear thought and objective reality. They are concerned with a reality which one senses—a sensational reality having many benefits of which we are presently deprived. We can sense connections between ourselves, our environment, our culture which bring us together through the sharing of patterns.

This relational way of viewing both self and culture provides a healing which automatically built into the Native and Eastern cultures instead of the modern Western system of taking people out of the culture and environment for healing. This modern reversal sets up a type of deprivation which works against healing. Detaching or separating in this way permeates our present systems and structures. Bateson sees it in the educational system: Children are taught at a tender age that the way to define something is by what it supposedly is in itself, not by its relation to other things. He stresses the importance of connecting patterns, of experiencing the world through relational definitions of people, objects and situations. He say:

> Is our reason for admiring a daisy the fact that it

> shows–in its form, in its growth, in its coloring and in its death–the symptoms of being alive? Our appreciation for it is, to that extent, an appreciation of its similarities to ourselves.[29]

Patterning also introduces the issue of creativity. The unconscious strives to create patterns out of formlessness.

> The ability to integrate and organize a pattern out of formlessness is an achievement which rational thought, being somewhat removed from its primitive being source and bound with habit and convention, may be incapable of doing...the reason that such a frontal attack often fails seems to be that the *free association* present in the unconscious is blocked in various ways and the really creative new relationships therefore are not seen.[30] (Sinnott)

4 MUSIC: The Mythic Artery

Despite the great difficulty in describing music through words, we have tended to divide ourselves into groups which have rather extreme attitudes about the subject. The first group is the analysts. These people are usually committed to describing music, musical experiences, musical response, in precise, logical and measurable terms. The most obvious way to keep music within these boundaries is to stick to formalized music theory as the source of all things connected with music. The form and structure of music contain beautiful examples of form and logic. Music and mathematics share similar concepts and principles. Within this sphere, music truly can be considered a science, reflecting scientific principles. This is part of the reassuring aspect of music. It does reflect the form and harmony in the universe. The danger comes in the over analysis of music.

Very few musical analysts have attempted to tackle the problem of maintaining the integrity of the scientific aspects of music while still giving equal consideration to the artistic and emotional side, which is in practical terms the side which most people experience. However, some theoreticians, musicologists, ethnomusicologists, and researchers into the psychology of music have made attempts.

Leonard B. Meyer, MacDonald Critchley and R. A. Hanson have made useful efforts to unite these two aspects of music—the analytical and the emotional. Meyer's books, *Emotion and Meaning in Music* and *Explaining Music,* represent the analysis of music with an effort to acknowledge and come to terms with the emotional response initiated by music. Although Meyer, in these two works is primarily analyzing music, he analyzes with reference to the effect on the total person. Critchley and Henson describe the scientific aspects of music in terms of its neurophysiological effects in the book *Music and the Brain.* This work considers some of the important findings on split-brain research and the importance of total brain functioning, especially the right brain hemisphere in musical activity.

One outstanding characteristic of Meyer, Critchley, and Henson is that they approach their subject matter with great humility, realizing the difficulty of the task and encouraging criticism and analysis. Meyer states that through his studies and explorations of individual pieces of music, he hopes to illuminate as fully as possible the source and basis of the power of music to engage and entrance us.

Another group of musicians, music lovers and even some music therapists refrain from discussing music in words because they feel that analysis takes away from the enjoyment and effect of music. This group, surprisingly enough, is not solely composed of people who would be considered emotional types. Quite often, the most intellectual types remain firm in this attitude. Music provides for them a release from words. The beauty of music is contained within this release. I have met doctors, physicists, mathematicians, psychiatrists and psychologists as well as many others whom I would consider to be analytical types, who would not touch the subject. The best answer might be the standard "chills up my spine" reply.

The one group which more consistently tries to balance the analytical and emotional sides of music is the group of composers and performers who write about music and about their lives with music, in autobiographical form. We have the letters of Beethoven, Tschaikowsky, Mahler, descriptions of music by John Cage, Leonard Bernstein, and hundreds of others. One representative of this group is Hindemith, with his book entitled *The Composer's World*. He aptly describes the dilemma of description and the rationale for our humility:

> The ultimate reason for this humility will be the musician's conviction that beyond all the rational knowledge he has amassed and all his dexterity as a craftsman, there is a region of visionary irrationality in which the veiled secrets of art dwell, sensed but not understood, implored but not commanded, imparted but not yielding. He cannot enter this region, he can only pray to be elected one of its messengers.[31]

These limitations of description seem to be a limitation of our Western tradition.

In the musical literature of India, Islam, China, Japan and other Eastern and mid-Eastern countries, the mysterious side of music is described at length. Some of these texts are laced with religious doctrine which we may or may not believe. However, these authors come close to defining and describing the essence of music. Perhaps it is because they do not feat violating the scientific aspects when exploring the spiritual, aesthetic and emotional aspects which play a large part in creating the mystery of music. Inayat Khan, the Sufi master, has written extensively on the mysteries of music. He speaks of music as a divine art because it is the exact miniature of the law working through the whole universe.

> Life depends upon the rhythmic working of the whole mechanism of the body. Breath manifests as voice, as word, as sound; and the sound is continually audible, the sound without and the sound within ourselves. That is music; there is music outside and within ourselves. Music inspires not only the soul of the great musician, but every infant which, the instant it comes into the world, begins to move its little arms and legs with the rhythm of music. Therefore it is no exaggeration to say that music is the language of beauty.[32]

To provide a comprehensive understanding of music, we need both Leonard Meyer and Inayat Khan.

The world of images, symbols and metaphors can provide a deeper understanding and, more important, a relational understanding of music. Although often only used as an aside, images are used by most of the people mentioned in the previous groups. Images are used by both Khan and Meyer. Meyer calls them extramusical, whereas Khan interprets them as being part of the music itself. In other words, *nothing is really extramusical. There are musical qualities in and around everything and everyone. Through this concept we are led to music as the Mythic Artery.*

We have already described the necessity for humans to find sources of renewal, restoration, revitalization. Our emotional, spiritual and physical resources become low at various stages of our lives, whether we are patients or not. The two primary sources described previously to help us renew our strengths were *creativity* and a symbolic *death-rebirth*. If we consider everything to be musical, music, or music therapy, would play an intimate part in this renewal and transformation process. It is up to each of us to identify the specific musical qualities contained within ourselves and our environment to accomplish this task. This would include our thoughts, our images, our situations and environment, our history, etc. This process of identifying and using music provides a unification and a connecting, in the healing sense described earlier by Bateson. We search, anticipate, appreciate, and bathe our consciousness in connections. In this way we do not necessarily eliminate suffering, pain, disease, misunderstanding, but rather we come to accept these things as part of the on-going process of life and try to find creative solutions whenever possible.

The Mythic Artery is an image, a way of thinking about music. which will aid us in our search for health. The Mythic Artery is liquid. It is vibrating. It is full of life-giving nutrients and chemicals. It quenches our thirst. It goes to and comes from the heart. It travels through all of time and contains the wisdom of the ages. It restores. It re-creates and cleanses. It brings us to the community of man and life as a whole. It gives us power, strength, humility. It is a stream which winds back through all the ages to the essence of our beginnings—our first heart beat, the first story of our existence. It allows us to be part of the whole and yet unique within the travelling undulations of time. It recycles. It purifies. It transforms. This is the music of life.

This is the true meaning of the expression that music is a universal language. Although many technicians of music criticize the use of this expression and prefer the theory that music is not universal because it is culturally derived, the notion that the whole of music unites us would be a feasible interpretation of the Mythic Artery and a Universal language.

Music stimulates our senses. And our senses permeate our whole being. It is very difficult to separate all the different ways in which music stimulates us. Researchers have attempted to isolate the variables to predict the influence of music on behavior. However, considering that images, symbolic associations, sound, which may not be monitored on laboratory equipment, will all stimulate and affect our senses, it is quite difficult to come up with laboratory tested theories which would have any relevance to practical, clinical environments.

We must learn to heighten our levels of perception toward healthy activity. For example, in a Music Therapy session, the therapist should use as many healing agents as possible and encourage clients to experience these influences to the depths of their experience, for them to receive and maintain the benefits. A music therapy session which taps into the Mythic Artery is a gestalt. There is no separating the complex aspects of the event or monitoring which stimulant has which effect. In most cases the effects are not immediately perceptible in behavior change, but rather constitute a deeper, soul-searching initiation for change which may only become visible in the long-term results. It is a move to encourage creativity and resourcefulness in the truest sense, that is, finding strength where there appears to be none and re-sourcing oneself or touching one's source again.

It is the job of the music therapist to provide some ritual which will allow the participants to accept the experience on a high and deep level of sense perception. The symbol or image or metaphor of the Mythic Artery need not be a conscious one for the participants. In fact, it does not necessarily have to be a conscious influence on the therapist. "The Mythic Artery" is merely the naming of a process which happens anyway, whether we care to acknowledge it or not.

In my work with psychiatric patients, I found that many of these participants would tap themselves into the musical mythical artery. It only took the smallest amount of primitive resourcefulness on their part. Patients actually came up with the mythic transformative themes on their own. The therapist only brought the music and a supportive atmosphere. The techniques themselves varied extensively. The message contained in this insight, for me, was that the human animal, though we are young, has a heritage of survival. The sickest person may find this heritage and use it as a source of renewal, if merely guided into the right direction.

Although we consider ourselves to be a highly-developed and sophisticated culture, our ancestors in time experienced many of our same basic tendencies. This is a fact to be used rather than discarded. In many ways we are the same as the Homo Erectus or the Australopithecines who roamed the savannahs searching for sustenance. We have the same feats of flood, famine, illness, war, survival. Myth is a connection to our past and our future.

In ancient times, myths served as a stabilizer within the culture, a sign that all things would pass and return again with different names, a connection to the past, a hope for the future. Myths told stories which balanced constancy and adaptability. The constancy was represented by the presence of indigenous cultural conventions, reference to history, the gods. Adaptability was represented by new situations—a scary journey, new and unfamiliar characters, a challenge in some task which seemed impossible, but was undertaken nevertheless. At the core of mythic events was transformation. The heroes would return or die, but always transformed in body and/or spirit, endowed with new gifts. An entire people would begin life again, but in a new land, becoming transformed within their new environment. With transformation, a type of death and rebirth are always implied. For this is the process of adaptability and change.

Music carries messages which speak of our intimate involvement in the human condition and connects us to the historical stream of human existence and all of Nature. For music is the expression which focuses on the continuity of life. This is the Mythic Artery.

Music as Metaphor and Symbol

Music as an expression functions as a metaphor and symbol of our experience. It captures and focuses on a certain feeling, a particular situation, a relationship, and proceeds to describe these things in pure sound without the interference of word symbols which must travel through complex intellectual pathways. I was once put in my place by a patient who understood this far better than myself.

I often struggle with the inclination to bridge a music therapy activity at the end through discussion, back to everyday life. Since each session is a journey into alternatives, I always feel I owe it to the patients to help them back through a transition and closure time, which usually takes the form of "talking" about how we feel.

Once I was questioning a patient about what his chant and drumbeat had meant. Like any good therapist, I found different ways of asking the question. I first asked directly what it meant. He said he didn't know. It just felt good to have done it. Then I probed a little deeper: "Can't you just give us a few words to describe how it felt, what it means to you now?" Then from the group another patient called out to me, "Lady, if he could say it, he wouldn't be singing it." I thought about that comment for a long time, and it helped me to have more respect for silence.

Of course it meant what it meant, and he had already told me what it meant by singing and drumming. His music was a symbolic representation of some aspect of his experience—pure and simple. It was also self-contained and complete.

It had already gone beyond words. It was an expression of clarity and communication. Everyone in the group had been moved. I had been moved. He said it had made him feel better. What better occasion for celebration in silence?

We paint sound pictures in music: My life is like this music, or my music is like a journey, or the sunrise is the music, or my music is my fear. We objectify our feelings, our situations. In this way they are expressed, which is one large step toward healing, and they are shared, which is a second large step toward healing. This can take place through playing a classical or jazz piece, spontaneous music or allowing a recorded piece to travel through to create our expression in poem, paint or clay. The technique does not make a lot of difference.

Expressing, then proceeding on to balance is a healing thing in itself. Much pain and disease could be prevented if we could only find adequate ways ot expressing ourselves. Obviously, words have limitations and do not always do the job. We are reminded of the saying "Music begins where words leave off." All the arts provide these necessary resources for expression. Throughout history most cultures have maintained rituals and ceremonies which provide opportunities for expressing and sharing their deepest thoughts, feelings, and beliefs through ritual forms. We have lost most of these communal opportunities. Although there are pockets of expressive ritual left in some communities, these are usually exclusive societies or churches and do not extend to the needs of mankind in general.

When we use the arts to create metaphors and symbols of our experience, we make an artifact or music which serves three main healing functions.

1) A work of art and music usually focus on one outstanding theme or message.

This differs from our usual inclination when we are in a state of need, that is, bombarded by mixed emotions, confused, indecisive. A piece of music focuses on pain, joy, anger, peace, frustration, satisfaction, confusion, clarity, at any given time, and usually develops that theme for awhile. It also dramatizes the qualities of the one experience or feelings for intensification. This gives the person a chance to deal with one emotion at a time and to feel the full depth of that emotion, rather than vacillating simultaneously from one to another.

2) An artistic expression is an objectification.

By participating in musical activities (and this includes listening, since we know our being is moved on every level, even in what may seem like stillness), we symbolically experience situations other than the one in which we presently find ourselves. Since music is an expression of the beliefs, feelings, attitudes of the times, when we hear music, in some significant way these beliefs, feelings and attitudes are passed on to us. They therefore represent alternatives. In this passage the patient/client "hears" new ideas for solutions, experiences new feelings, is re-assured by "sounds" which complement and re-affirm his or her own feelings.

In Baroque music we are re-assured about order and return, In the music of Bach, we learn that the same theme can have many variations without destroying the integrity of the original theme. In the music of the Shakuhachi, we float and drift through gardens and streams and experience the coolness of water, the scampering of tiny birds. We are inspired to ask: Is that me? Is that the depth of my love? In this way, one appreciates what should be retained and examines ways of changing any negative or destructive influence. To hear one's own improvised music played back on tape, or receive the reaction of a group audience can often be a surprise and shock. Secrets come through the music which may never have been expressed before.

3) Of course, the third healing benefit is to find out that you are not alone. You are not isolated from the ongoing

processes of life. Others share the same fears and throughout time have experienced the same myths. This is the healing benefit of connections.

We see that we are connected. The processes of life, of nature, the situations, the patterns, the shapes, textures, colors, sounds of life are shared without restrictions of time or space. We see also that appreciating these connections is a health-creating and health-maintaining activity. Music is a celebration of these connections.

Very few people allow themselves this expressive privilege. Yet in the end, expressive metaphor, symbol and medicine are equally essential to the health of man.

Music as Tension and Resolution

Since the process of tension and resolution symbolizes death-rebirth and since death-rebirth represents change, just as music is change, a great deal of our discussion of the structure of music will consider the tension-resolution processes as reflected in music.

The relationship between the Death-Rebirth Myth and Tension-Resolution in music is one of reflection. The music reflects the myth, and vice versa. In practical terms, the music serves as a vehicle for the myth, placing the myth in time and space by providing it with a living, symbolic form. This can happen through the structure of the music. Music expresses the myth by making it available through sense perception. In a way it solidifies myth and gives it a workable form. In this way myth travels to us through music.

One of the basic considerations in musical composition is the concept of tension and resolution. Most musical compositions contain the process of tension and resolution within all the elements. One or several of the components of the piece "build up" to a climax point, then resolve. This is also the pattern taken by many life situations. We experience a type of transformation through a peak experience or feeling. This life movement can be applied to any number of circumstances. Each day can be considered a series of transformations through our various activities, or as the many overlapping motifs in some musical piece. One's entire life might have one major transformation. Or both of these circumstances may happen simultaneously. There may be many peaks, climaxes, transformations within one life.

The idea that a type of giving over and loss must occur, in order for change or growth to be accomplished, constitutes the connection to myth. The musical symbol serves as an example of regeneration, renewal, building and transformation. It does not deny the passion inherent in these encounters. Rather, it acknowledges the tensions of pain, anger, hate, melancholy, confusion, frustration, hurt, despair and the resolution of joy, love, fulfillment, clarity, hope. *Musical encounters allow the passion or feeling to become externalized, therefore providing form.*

One initial example will illustrate. A composer who clearly manifests the death-rebirth myth through musical tension and resolution is Chopin, especially in his etudes and preludes. His Prelude in E Minor provides a simple example. The tension-resolution process in melody builds and resolves once in the prelude. The music builds to one point of transformation, one climax, in which death and rebirth occur in the same moment. The movement changes from moving away from the tonal focus to a point which leads toward tonic.

At the point of transformation, one chord, or one moment in time and space, there is a resolution of the tension produced by the previous 15 measures.

Levi-Strauss discusses the relationship between music and myth. He states: Music and myth are both structural and untranslatable. Each holds a basic dichotomy. They also

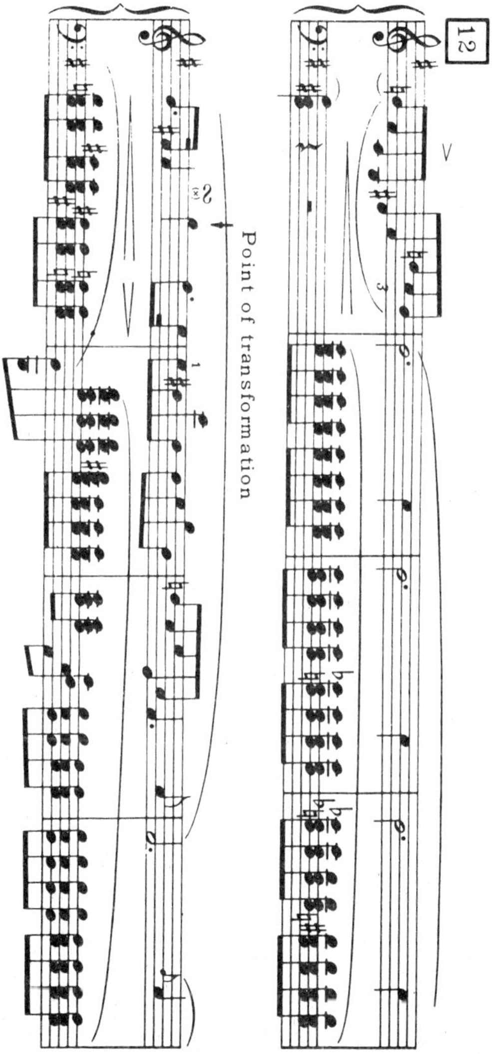
12
Point of transformation

hold themes and counter themes which can be changed into an infinite variety.[33]

The point made by Levi-Strauss in reference to the dichotomies existing in music and myth are particularly relevant to the death-rebirth myth. Music and myth both acknowledge and accept paradox. The point of transformation in Chopin's E minor prelude represents both death and rebirth in the same chord, moment or space. Both exist together and become one another. For at the moment of rebirth, another death has in fact begun.

These mythical, musical patterns often manifest themselves despite the avowed intention of the composer. The death-rebirth myth is contained in a Bach Fugue, the simplicity of a Gregorian chant, the complexity of a Beethoven sonata, and the primitive life force trance of Mick Jaegger's "Brown Sugar." There is no need to sacrifice our rich Western musical tradition in search of myth.

Levi-Strauss's example of this lack of intention is Ravel and his classic "Bolero", a repetitious building of tensions and resolutions. It is known that Ravel never took the piece seriously, considered it "empty of music" and was extremely surprised at its popularity. This brings up the possibility of myth travelling through composers without their knowledge. Myths can be reflected in music without intent on the part of the composer. The structure and patterns of the music are available to communicate myth whether program music or not. Although Levi-Strauss does not discuss this possibility, he considers the relationship between music and myth one of analogy within their common structural patterning. He is interested in the pattern-forming nature of the mind. Patterning again becomes an important consideration.

Music as Patterns

> ...the first step in explaining the meaning of musical patterns is the fact that they are translated in the brain into general lingua franca of all other patterns—mental patterns such as grief, expectation, fear, desire and so forth, and bodily patterns such as hunger, pain, retention, sexual excitement, any of the tensions associated with a raising of the adrenalin level in the blood—and the corresponding resolutions—allow us to see the similarities between the musical patterns and those more personal ones which form the constant undercurrent of our thought.[34] (Terence McLaughlin)

Patterns of tension-resolution, melodic and rhythmic motifs and themes, repetitions, compositional forms, dynamics all combine to weave complex patterns in sound. Pitch, time and volume are the key modes which utilize and communicate tension-resolution patterns. Within these three modes we experience the elements of music: melody, harmony, rhythm, meter, timbre, dynamics and texture. In a musical composition these modes often inter-relate, setting up complex crossings of patterns.

The appreciation of patterns is an aesthetic experience. Even though people may not be aware of the theory and concepts of musical composition, they nevertheless do experience the feeling of patterns in the music. The musical patterning establishes a connection and relevance to their being through common patterns. In other words, as a person hears musical patterns he identifies or associates with the patterns, whether consciously or unconsciously, which share a common theme or movement of his life or being. He hears cycles of giving and taking, aggression and tenderness, a peak experience and a period of rest.

He hears pain and pleasure, loss and birth. The music may suggest pictures or concrete situations from the past or fantasies of the future. The overall effect is: "I am the music" or "I am like the music," or at least that "Music is like a part of me." So the music has a deep connecting influence on man in that it expresses and symbolizes patterns of the human condition.

A pattern usually suggests a process. Here the therapy goes into full action. As long as there is a connecting pattern and process, there is hope. This patterning identification is an aesthetic perception and experience. It is difficult to know when and where in our society we lost our overall value for beauty. The concrete idea that beauty can bring healing, would be considered useless, a frill, a token gesture, on the back wards of most medical and psychiatric treatment institutions. And yet the human animal longs for beauty as much as we long for life and breath. We need it as much as the air, food, light, shelter. *If we are unable to experience beauty in concrete ways, we will surely die.*

The concept that the human life is born to seek beauty is a substantial ingredient to a healthy existence and goes beyond medical treatment. It is in a sense the step before and the step after. A great deal of illness, pain and suffering can be both endured and fought if a deeper meaning for this pain has been identified. A meaning, again, which goes beyond analytical and intellectual interpretations and which touches the whole human—the soul of man—which is the representative of our body, mind, heart, psyche, emotions, hopes and fears.

Patterns reach these depths. The patterns in music remind us of our connections to the whole of life. They do not allow us to alienate ourselves. Furthermore, they reassure us about the on-going processes of life as a whole, and the significance of each life within that whole. This aesthetic connecting constitutes a step towards meaning in life—which is, after all, the only reason man wants to live and subsequently endure any suffering at all.

Music as Rhythm in Life

Rhythm is one of the strongest components of music. A great deal of music is based solely on rhythmic constructs or perhaps one slight pitch variation with different sized drums. Rhythm is the central aspect of most African and aboriginal, Island and Native American Indian music. Although rattles, shakers and other percussive sounds may be added with various pitch differentiation, several drums provide either a drone effect or repetitive rhythmic patterns. Often chants are added to these rhythmic patterns which serve to develop the ritual ceremonies. These chants also often have complex patterns. However, the drum remains as the vital carrier of the basic rhythmic message.

The drum was invented by early man to communicate messages to fellow humans beyond the distance range of normal, everyday sound. The drum had two primary functions:

1) It was an attempt to extend the sphere of communication for reasons of survival;
2) It was an attempt to connect men to fellow men.

All of the first instruments—primarily drums and horns—were used for these purposes. Music, when played on these most primitive instruments, expressed and communicated the most basic and primitive needs of the early men. This was the beginning of the Mythic Artery. We have, in fact, invented a musical tradition which began with the first chant, the first drum beat, the first sound from a crude horn. In the evolution of the thousands of musical traditions, which may be considered indigenous cultural forms, we are all still connected across time and space to these primitive beginnings and all of our music contains these primitive beginnings despite the layers of development we have superimposed over the centuries. Although we may consider our music to be sophisticated and civilized, in its essence it must retain this primitive core. For a tree does not disregard its core over the years, even though it receives layers of new growth. Rather, the core remains as the center and the food route for the entire structure.

Within our culture we tend to think of our development in hierarchal terms. When we have achieved a new stage, we discard the previous stages, or at least consider the latest acquisition of greatest value. When a child becomes an adult, she must forget the childlike knowledge, for it is inferior. We often forget that our beginnings are an integrated and vital part of our now's. We must constantly be aware of our primitive or more basic needs and resources as we develop and refine our intellectual needs and resources.

Through this channel we are connected to the first man who played the first drum. We are the first drum player.

This brings up the most controversial issue of musical taste and "The Devil's Music". Throughout the development of music, from time to time a form will emerge which is considered to be "The Devil's Music." This has happened as early as the Renaissance and Baroque periods. It was one of the reasons for the establishment of the provisions of musica ficta, to protect church music from evil influences. Prior to these periods, the Greeks and Romans had strict rules about which modes were good and which were evil, which instruments were good and which were evil. The Chinese lute players fraternity had extremely rigid rules about the when's, where's and how's of lute playing, even the who's, in order to protect the player and the populace from the lower instincts or evil influences.

Strauss, Beethoven and hundreds of other innovative composers were accused of evil influences. Very often these culprit influences were classified as the rhythmic elements.

On the more contemporary modern scene, the Devil's Music has been known to include Jazz, Soul, Rock, Blues, and most recently, Punk Rock and Disco. Most of these idioms contain the strong influences of Black rhythmic pulse. Regardless of the multitude of harmonic and melodic structures which separate and classify these forms, when much of this music is stripped down to the rhythmic content, we hear the rhythmic pulse: Mick Jaegger's "Brown Sugar," the Pointer Sisters' "How Long," the voodoo music of Haiti, Art Blakey's "Tobi Ilu," the music of the Sun Dance. It is most often the main message of the music. And what is this important message which travels through such a great variety of music across oceans and centuries? It is the beat. We must have the beat, the heartbeat. We must know the pulse of life and experience it it through dance, through music, to re-affirm our own rhythmic existence from the first drummer to ourselves.

Sometime ago Dr. Hajime Murooka put together a record entitled "Lullaby from the Womb." It was a popular record, advertised in the windows of most pop and rock record stores. Retailers had a hard time keeping it on the shelf.

One side of the record was the actual sound of what the unborn child hears in the mother's womb prior to birth–the sound of the main artery. The other side contained classical pieces, half of which were superimposed over these natural sounds and then the same classical pieces with the same rhythmic meter, without the sounds of the mother's body.

The original pure sounds from the mother's body were

strong, loud, and intense. The classical pieces were:

Meditation from "Thais" (Massenet)
Air on a G String (Bach)
Intermezzo from "Cavalleria Rusticana" (Mascagni)
The Swan from "Carnival of the Animals" (Saint Saens)
Andante Cantabile (Tchaikovsky)
Panorama from "Sleeping Beauty" (Tchaikovsky)
Traumerei from "Scenes from Childhood" (Schumann)
"Jewels of the Madonna" (Wolf-Ferrqui)

Dr. Morooka's point was that these sounds form an intimate part of the unborn child's world. He recommended that, if a baby is fussy and distraught, this record would help to calm him. In his experiments, this worked with 99% of the babies.

When I am listening to most disco music and disregard all the Hollywood, the lyrics, the hysteria and repetitious melodic forms, what comes to me as the strong, positive element of this music is the same rhythmic pulse as Bach's Air in G, with more intensity.

Many people, including myself, have complained about the starving quality of popular music today. But the point remains that it is popular. It is a statement from the culture, as music is an expression and reflection of the culture. Accepting it for this reason, we must sincerely try to identify the value of the music through its message. What is the music saying? What does it mean?

The music is saying: Let the heart beat. This is all we have left–a heart beat, one Massive mythic, rhythmic stream which connects us vitally to life. And the beat goes on. Let us feel and experience this connection, these instincts, the beginnings. Let the juices flow. The beat of life must go on if we are to survive.

What is the message of punk rock—an existential vacuum and an important message. No tranformative vision for the future, but one solid statement: The heart continues to beat. This is all we have left. Reflect. We are stripped down to our bare bones. All we have left is a heartbeat. Can we not now build from a heart beat to accept and incorporate our primitive beginnings into the rituals of our lives—to celebrate and dance the Heartbeat. This is the Life Force of Rhythm within the mythic artery.

Rhythm and other time factors are realized through sound, silence, duration, tension and resolution.

Music as Time Tensions

Time tensions are realized through tempo and meter, divisions of even duration. There is a universal tendency towards simple time units of two, three and four steady beats across musical traditions. Any departure from the normal pulse of the music comes as a point of tension, e.g., when there are five, seven or eleven beats in the bar, syncopated rhythm (where expected accent is displaced) and cross-rhythm effects. The possibilities for creation of tension become even more complicated with the interplay between pitch and time.

Another consideration in the creation of time tension is the effect of rhythmic repetition in production of a trance state or altered state of consciousness. The trance effect has been discussed by many, among them George Leonard in *The Silent Pulse* and William Johnston in *Silent Music*.

The physical effects of music, associated to a great extent with rhythmic tensions, have been documented by many. Studies agree on the following conclusions on the physiological effects of music:

1) increase or decrease of metabolic rate;
2) increase or decrease of muscular energy;
3) acceleration or deceleration in breathing and increase or decrease in its regularity;
4) marked but variable effect on blood volume, pulse and blood pressure;
5) a lowering of the threshold for sensory stimulation of different modes.

The repetition of a rhythmic pattern can suggest a type of transformation through a trance-like state. In other words, tension is created not so much through deviation in regularity of beat, but rather through a contrast between a normal functioning state of consciousness, experienced prior to adjustment to repetitious rhythmic patterning, and different or altered state of consciousness produced by that particular rhythmic pattern and its repetition. A person maintains a regular or normal state of consciousness. Through experiencing repetitious rhythmic patterning, one travels to and through an altered or transformed state of consciousness. At a certain point the music ends, the rhythmic, trance-inducing stimulus is removed, and a person returns to the normal functioning state. This can constitute a death-rebirth or transformative experience.

Musical examples of this type of rhythmic activity are obvious in all of the forms mentioned above. Much of this music combines rhythm for a syncopation effect.

The actual workings of the rhythmic patterns may be simple or complex. However, the basic pulse concept remains. Regardless of the theoretical aspects or complexity, the average person experiences the stimulation of rhythmic pulse. Regardless of our musical taste and preference, this rhythmic pulse, this Life Force, endures as a valuable resource for the overall health of man in his quest for survival.

Music as Life Breath

We have forgotten how to breathe. Millions of Westerners are learning how to breathe again through the practice of yoga—taking in the prana or Life Breath. Thousands more are learning to breathe in clincs of psycho-therapists through relaxation techniques. Even in dance studios and books on running,athletes and dancers have to be reminded to breathe.

The Chinese word ch'i is difficult to translate. It means vital breath, spirit, life. The Chinese say that in order for a work of art or music to have value, it must contain ch'i. Music, the Mythic Artery, brings us this vital breath through the forms of melody and harmony. We breathe in the tone and it brings us vital psychic resources which bring strength and cleanse as the prana, as the ch'i. We need to breathe the music into our lungs, into our blood stream, for health's sake. Mozart's "Andante Concerto No. 21 in C Major for Piano and Orchestra", Pachelbel's "Canon", the music of the Shachuhachi, the pure melody of Gregorian chants, Oregon's "Appear and Become", John McLaughlin's "Goal's Beyond"—these pieces of music flow into us as air, bringing renewal and refreshment. They are a transfusion of fresh air. Whereas the rhythmic beat is solid, the melody and harmony undulate, cross, meet. They are liquid. They vibrate in pitch variation. We soak up their messages, patterns, tensions, resolutions, contrasts, much as we absorb air and water.

Pitch tensions include melody (intervallic tensions and resolutions) and harmony (tonal tensions and resolutions). An intervallic tension represents the distance between two or more consecutive notes. A tonal tension represents the distance between two or more notes played simultaneously. Both of these tensions seek eventual resolution. In general, a tonal melody seeks a resolution of returning to the tonic note, after building a series of ''near'' resolutions by returning to other tones in the tonic chord, such as the third or fifth. The tonal tensions seek some combinations of the tonic chord as a resolution. These pitch patterns are ''archtypical patterns.'' The series of unresolved tensions are unconsummated until they do, in fact, resolve to tonic. Atonal music does not follow these tendencies. However, quite often, atonal music does invent equally predictable rules which build tension and strive for resolution, e.g., Schoenberg's tone row.

A need for ultimate resolution builds as the false resolutions to a third or fifth, or other steps on a scale build more and more tension and anticipation. This may occur over the length of the entire piece, i.e., a melodic line would never return to the tonic until the end of a piece. Or it may occur in the form of repetition of motifs, phrases, or a rondo or bar form, i.e., a resolution to tonic comes many times.

An example of both intervallic tension-resolution and tonal tension-resolution and the interplay between melody and harmony is illustrated in Yusef Lateef's ''Lowland Lullaby''. It is a simple duet between flute and bass. It provides slow melodic movement by the flute and harmonic movement by bass, each return separately several times to tonic, but culminate in a tonal resolution with the flute and bass both returning to tonic simultaneously. This is the point of transformation.

Volume tensions and resolutions are perhaps the most obvious to hear. They take the form of dynamics, timbre, texture in a piece. Dynamics are manifested in the p, pp, ppp, pppp (degrees of softness) and the f, ff, fff, ffff (degrees of loudness) or crescendos and diminuendos. A simplified example of how the tension may build and resolve would be

f, ff, fff, ffff, p, pp, ppp, pppp

The 4f represents the point of transformation. The dynamics of a piece are rarely this simple, and, again, usually constitute a series of dynamic tensions and releases. The more subtle effects of volume come through the interpretation of timbre or color and texture of a piece. These elements are often left to the discretion of the artist playing the piece. However, one piece which dramatically embodies the mythical, musical forms in all their complexity and all their simplicity is Samuel Barber's "Adagio for Strings", which illustrates a beautiful interplay between pitch, time, and volume. It is a long piece which gradually builds in volume to one intense peak with full strings in unison (adding the pitch element, a change in direction toward tonic) in a full fortissimo. Barber strikingly employs a full rest after this intense climax before savouring the resolution in degrees of softness. This piece communicates the death-rebirth myth in the fullest sense.

It is extremely difficult to disengage the complex webs of musical patterning, and this task is better undertaken by theoreticians, analysts, and musicologists. However, for our purpose a small amount of analysis will aid overall understanding of the joint functioning of myth and music. Perhaps the ability to extract the important pattern from a wealth of extraneous detail, to see the essentials of a situation stripped of superficial differences,and to generalize from experiences is a key to the whole coherency of our mental life.

Musical elements of tension-resolution become symbolic representations of some of the most basic life processes. They provide a reminder of our common and profound collective condition. The processes of nature, life, death, suffering, release are remembered and experienced symbolically within music. The music, as the vehicle to myth, becomes as well, the bridge between the preventative and curative powers of myth and the concrete situations of life.

Music as Healing

Sufi Inyat tells us:

> ...health is a condition of perfect rhythm and tone. And what is music? Music is rhythm and tone. When the health is out of order, it means the music is out or order. In all the occupations of life where beauty has been the inspiration, where the divine wine has been poured out, there is music.[35]

This summarizes the Sufi philosophy regarding the healing powers of music. Music is life and health, a reflection of the grand scheme, divine itself. Many ancient cultures have used music as a healer. Certain processes and qualities inherent in music have healing potential, as we have seen. Beyond the organizational aspects of music, there are more general considerations into the healing powers of music as used in Music Therapy.

The first is magic, or mystery, or perhaps the divine and spiritual aspect of music so often ignored in a clinical setting. The magical side of music complements the clinical side. Unfortunately the words magic (in the anthropological sense), mystery, divine and spiritual do not get a positive response in clinical settings. However, there are other places within our culture where such concepts are accepted. The most obvious example is within a religious context. It's acceptable to hear voices, or speak in tongues in some situations. In other places, hearing voices or speaking in tongues becomes a symptom and a sign for increase of medication. To the Navaho, music is both a vehicle to and a celebration of our divine collective nature. The Indian does not know that the magic of music will bring healing, instead he trusts that it will. The cultural difference emerges in the distinction between known and unknown.

We find magic wherever the element of chance and accident and the emotional play between hope and fear have a wide and extensive range. We do not find magic whenever the pursuit is certain, reliable and well under the control of rational methods and technological processes. Within our cultural context, one of the vehicles for magic is religion and for science, therapy. This separation between religion and therapy has taken us to our present unmagical state. Within the various therapeutic methodologies sanctioned by most of the medical community, magic is denied for the following reasons: 1) it cannot be observed; 2) it often cannot be analyzed or understood; 3) it often implies spiritual or psychic functioning levels; 4) it cannot be defined; 5) most important, it takes us to levels of depth for which there are no word symbols. No matter how illusive, it is still there. Music affects most people subjectively. It can also affect people objectively, but within the subjective reactions the magic is found. It conveys symbolic meanings which are difficult to describe in verbal language and are intimately tied to our emotions. In some ways, the symbolic meanings of music are similar to verbal language, but one difference is the immediate power of music to move on an emotional level. It directly affects our feelings, those human reactions which reside in the subjective parts of man's being, perhaps part of right brain hemisphere activity.

A second characteristic often neglected is the aesthetic

nature of musical experience. Music fulfills man's need for beauty, and can satisfy his search for meaning in the world. Many administrators, doctors, teachers, nurses, therapists, and some music therapists do not realize that aesthetic experience can have a preventative and curative effect. They do not value the use of arts in therapy. Sometimes they have not been encouraged by society to develop their own artistic drives. Occasionally they may pursue artistic endeavors in their private lives, but classify art as play and therapy as work, therefore leaving out this important vehicle for healing. One of the basic premises for the music therapist is that everyone is an artist, but society dictates that the living, working stuff of art is for "the artist", a person removed and socially trained. In many older cultures, leisure time was not a time for meaningless activity. Leisure time was time given to aesthetic experiences such as playing or listening to music. When native and traditional cultures made music, danced and costumed, they were usually performing rituals necessary for the health and well-being of the community, coming together to express their beliefs and feelings about life. These activities were intimately tied to man's search for meaning. The average Navaho male spends 75% of his time in ceremonials and rituals. Our culture does not maintain these aesthetic values for the average man or the patient in the psychiatric ward, or the cerebral palsied child. Many of our treatments ignore the problem of man's search for meaning, only encouraging the return of alienation. These methods deal with changes on a superficial level, only what is seen, or can be observed by an outsider. Often behavior is a reflection of one's inner being. But it cannot be assumed that it is the total picture of man, or the only part which merits a response.

Aesthetics tends to be somewhat neglected. It's difficult to define and resides largely in that grey right hemisphere.

Aesthetic experiences are unique and personal. Aesthetics is interdisciplinary and crosses lines of values, beliefs, personality qualities, perception skills, education, attitudes. But through aesthetic experience it is possible for each man to find his own frame of reference for the universe. Through valuing beauty, one can find ways of absorbing strength from the world in which one lives. In a music therapy session, the tunes or expressions may not always sound beautiful to a critic; however,the music therapist hears these expressions as profound representations of human experience. Through the profundity comes beauty—an artist's symbolization through sound of the basic elements which make up life experience—pain, sorrow, joy, sadness, loss, rebirth. If accepted with this attitude, such primitive expressions can form the foundation for a positive attitude toward life for a person disabled in any way. The client and therapist work together to create and experience beauty. They find symbolic forms, patterns, shapes, textures in improvised music which convey significant meanings. They hear healing themes in recorded pieces which transfer to life outside the music therapy session.

The third healing consideration in music therapy sessions is the natural ability of music to provide experiences in the creative processes. As mentioned earlier, Jung considered creativity one of man's basic instincts. It can be implied from his theory that all men not only have the potential to develop creativity in some area, to some degree, but also that everyone has a drive to be creative which must be satisfied. This drive can create products beneficial both to the individual and to society if the proper channels are discovered. If the creative instinct is not used or properly channeled, it can have a harmful effect on both. Even though music may not be the natural vehicle for everyone's creativity, it can be an experimental ground in which to try out creative processes and apply them through a powerful medium. Creative processes can be applied to anything. The music therapist offers opportunities for a person to try alternatives in problem-solving, have corrective experience in communication and learn about new sources of regeneration and enrichment and develop new skills. The music therapist combines resources for maximum benefit to all, or in other words, creates the most beautiful art work. All participants engage in a journey to discover the right sound quality, shape or color which describes and symbolizes an important part of the beings in the session and which other kinds of symbols cannot adequately describe and communicate. The good therapist leaves adequate space and time for the clients to fulfill their own creative process as part of the creation. Many therapists and methods presume they have all the knowledge about where and how a person must be healed. Many forms of therapy dictate exactly the way a person must alter behavior, attitude and mood to conform with the culture. Within creativity there is a way to adapt to the culture and express one's uniqueness, if clients have a safe place in which to experiment. The Mythic Artery provides such a place.

If music provides a vehicle for the myth, ritual creates a context for any subsequent mythical, musical event. At its most basic level ritual is defined as a prescribed form or method for the performance of religious or solemn ceremony. From the tone of this definition we can assume that ritual would be a serious and meaningful event. The ritual performance relates strongly to the cultural and social context, which in fact would be the object of a music therapy session. Ritual without carryover into the practical concerns of day-to-day life would hold little meaning.

> ...many rituals derive their power to transform identities and contexts of action and meaning, which are located in

> the mundane order of everyday life, through effecting transformations within the organization of their performance...[36] (Kapferer)

Ritual relates to the realities which are built around it, and which continue in their processes after the completion of a ritual performance. Of course, this is the intended result of a Music Therapy session, that through symbolic associations and performance of some type, clients will become transformed not only within the context of the ritual or session, but within situations in their lives as well.

Another important point made by Kapferer is that the transformation of a context must involve a transformation of its constituent elements. This is effected by these elements being related in ways different from their relation in a context in which they were previously constituted. In terms of a Music Therapy session, this may mean a rearrangement of constituents, an addition or subtraction of constituents, changing the quality of certain elements. The ritual provides a different perspective as well as new information. The key to this simultaneous or contingent transformation is found in objectification of problems, or illness, or even more specifically an externalization. Problems or illness receive a concrete form through performance.

This idea of transformation of context through the power of ritual relates directly to the mythical, musical framework, since the death-rebirth myth rests at the base of transformation.

As a ritualist the music therapist must develop respect for both convention and spontaneity. The ritual provides a basic structure which should be specific, reassuring and supportive, but not inhibitive to the individual needs of the participants.

The human spirit at its most basic level desires to be healed A person will identify with the healing elements of music and ritual and venture towards growth and transformation. Music is only a reflection of man himself. In this sense music will not violate the impulses of man but provide instead a framework from which to make choices.

PART II

MYTHICAL MUSICAL RITUAL

5 PRACTICE OF MUSICAL RITUAL

One of the original purposes of ritual in ancient civilizations was to order the life of the community in harmony with the forces of nature. We presently need this type of ritual in our daily lives. We have lost these forms which remind us of our place in the order of all things. Music reminds us. The four elements in ritual and music which encourage harmonic insight are: 1) patterns, 2) processes, 3) images, and 4) symbols.

Patterns, processes and symbols have all been discussed in relation to music and myth. Images provide another necessary link in this healing journey. Images come to us to suggest processes and patterns. Images become symbols. Therefore the materials of Music Therapy take on a significance. It is important to use materials which will inspire and create meaningful images.

It is also important, especially in groups or in the first stages of individual work, to employ a great variety of materials, to encourage a variety of images. The quality of materials is extremely important. For example, it is better to have fewer instruments of better quality, fewer paints of richer tone, than a large number of poor quality tools.

The idea of "image" itself must be expanded to include more than visual image. A sound image may be equally important.

Although music used alone is powerful, it can be even more effective with the addition of one or more other arts. This combination merely increases the possibilities for expression. In groups, such a combination offers a wider choice of resources.

In some cases recorded music suggests use of a particular medium. For example, some pieces suggest color and painting, some movement, some poetry or writing. To work with this musical suggestion gives the entire ritual a solid balance. The music therapist may use the same piece of music two or three times in one session, once to movement, once to poetry, once with clay.

Some people experience synaesthesia, or perceiving in several sensory modes simultaneously. For example, a person may hear a C-chord and see red, and have an accompanying smell as well. Synaesthesia may be a multi-mode which is possible for more people. This type of integration can be useful if given the variety of materials needed to express multi-dimensional perceptions.

In working with groups of individuals on a long-term basis, the use of various art materials may help to develop imagination in cycles of sessions which may end with a session in musical improvisation. Some people claim they do not have an imagination. Of course, everyone has an imagination. It is just a matter of developing and using it for health. The textures and colors of our materials can aid in this development.

The following descriptions are examples of Music Therapy which have been done with patients and Music Therapy students. Each session was a journey—a mythical, musical ritual which employed the arts to describe the patterns, processes and symbols of the healing journeys of many people. Every Music Therapy session is a journey, whether it be an initiation, a vision quest, a dream. For it should end in knowledge, corrective experience, and insight, thus change and transformation.

Music and Sand

Sand complements the music. It can be warm or cold, solid or liquid. It takes on form with water and human hands. It is the earth and the touching of the earth heals. Sand is malleable. It also carries the mythical messages through thousands of journeys in sand paintings and deserts of wind-blown dunes. It contains the smell of the sea and washes into the shore, yet does not resist when water calls it back. Sand is timeless and forever.

THE RITUAL

Participants were asked to: "Breathe deeply. Experience the quiet. Relax. Let yourself find a feeling of nothingness in the quiet. When the music begins, play with the dry sand. Think of the music as coming into the sand through your hands."

The music was "Hergest Ridge", by Mike Oldfield (21 minutes). After the music was over, participants were asked to complete their sand sculptures and come together in a circle for discussion. One person would describe his sculpture and each, in turn, selected another person to do the same. Each participant was given as much time as needed to describe the work. If someone could not find words to describe a sculpture, she was not persuaded to do so.

Some of the verbal responses one week later were:

exploration
playfulness
movement
floating
building
fun
secret
mysticism
travelling
pain
space
openness
the onset of genesis
strength
connections
moving up
melting
joyous
security
comfort
trust
permission to explore
develop and change
lightness
unobtrusiveness

Other extended responses were as follows:

a) It was a total experience–sand and music creation. It was positive and energy-giving. The experience of building parts of me in the sand has stayed with me and brought some "hidden" parts of me closer to the surface.

b) My words for my sand piece were: Paths coming from different places converging together to go up the mountain peak. A cave to shelter in and holes to hide in, from life, but a path leading out to the mountain.

c) The feeling evoked by the sand–the touch of its coolness, the memories consciously and unconsciously were called up through that touch to play a big part in the experience. They helped to lead into myself–to forget and find myself.

d) The sand! I have never felt so drawn to and connected with any other material to date. It was all-consuming. The music was both incidental and yet fundamental to my experience. Incidental because I was already one with the sand; fundamental, as I was aware of some aspects of it (e.g., floating sequence) which directly influenced the way I interacted with the sand.

e) My sand sculpture was "Intermingling, Boundaries, the Sea".

f) My piece was "Mountains and Valleys".

EXPLANATION OF RITUAL

It is obvious that the sand became a powerful vehicle for most participants. In this particular session, the music was intended to be a subtle, shaping influence which people could travel through, but which would not inhibit any unique interpretations or forms which might emerge outside the musical suggestion. It was meant to create a dream-like effect. The experience was intended to be a solitary, introspective task, but with time left for discussion and sharing.

The suggestion of "nothingness" was intended to inspire a sort of temporary death in order to find life. The suggestion of the music travelling through oneself to the sand was so that one could lose oneself in order to find oneself.

The music contained many overlapping motifs of tension and resolution. The sand represented nature. Instructions were simple, and given in a spirit and form of ritual, with respect for the materials and the silence of beginning.

Music and Shadow

Shadow responds to music. It is the secret side, the quiet, hidden side. It can be the dark side we mask so easily—evil, fear, sorrow, pain. It can also be hidden joy and exhuberance. It is self but not self—an intermediary puppet, with whom to play for awhile. It is clear—no features, only black against white. It brings clarity. It is magic. It cries. It touches another without touching flesh, as a symbol of encounter. It teases. It can fight when we cannot. It cannot hide the dance within us. It is quiet, but speaks of "other" things than words. It is a child who never played, a baby who was never rocked. It is death and birth. It is larger than life, smaller than a seed. Without the shadow, there is no light.

THE RITUAL

We combined shadow dancing with musical improvisation. A large theatrical spot light was reflected onto a blank, white wall. All other lights were turned off. A variety of musical instruments were set up in an orchestra form. Instruments included timpani, bass drum, bongos, two pianos, bell tree, gong, flutes, cello, string bass, violin, silver flute, guitar and tambourine. Participants were also encouraged to use their voices in musical improvisation. Instructions were as follows:

"Form two groups. Those who feel like being alone, and those who feel like being together. Those of you who are "together-feeling" form groups of pairs, threes, or larger amongst yourselves. Today we work with the shadow. Become aware of your shadow side–perhaps the dark side or secret side of yourself–whatever "shadow" suggests. Each person or group will have a turn creating a shadow dance. Start from a state of stillness or nothingness.Select a person or persons from the group to improvise to your dancing. If you wish you may tell them which instruments to play. Instrumentalists follow the dance or dancers, reflecting their movement in your music. If you need more of a musical direction, think of making an "undulating" sound.

Each shadow dance and improvisation was discussed by the performers immediately after the piece was completed. Group members were encouraged to share feelings of what it meant for them.

Some of the responses a week later:

mystery
chaos
wind
joy
struggling
expanded
no contact
aggression
invitation
present but withheld
spooky
togetherness
playful

death-rebirth
testing
freedom
peace
distance
love
the music was me
a struggle between two parts of myself
it simultaneously enveloped me and was absorbed by me

Responses to the question: Which instruments inspired you?

a) Spooky voices and cello.
b) The music supported me and allowed me to throw away things.
c) The tensions and releases in the music affected me along with the silences and breaks. The instruments very much matched my mood and feelings. I felt as one with the music.
d) The gentleness and warmth in the flute sound, cello and bass.
e) Beginning and exploring sounds, of flute, dancing and twirling of percussion. I felt the driving energy of the congo right through me. The music was for me and in me at the same time—my body became one with it.
f) I was struck by a sense of support.
g) An interflow between dancers and musicians.
h) The polarities of sound produced by flute/tone bass and guitar/bongos. The long breath of the flute inspired me, calmed me, opened me. The bongos instigated movement-agitation and direction.
i) Perfection otherwise because it did not disturb my flow.

j) It was a stretching feeling, the interaction between the music and my shadow, urging growth, building.

Other extended responses were:

a) I felt I could let loose and be supported by the music.
b) I found this to be extremely powerful activity and the things which happened were meaningful. Playing for others to move also had a great deal of meaning for me which was extra to my own moving. It was not an easy activity for me to do, but was beneficial. At one point, I almost didn't complete the activity, but am glad I decided to do so, and finished for myself. I felt a lot of support from the music in that I trusted people playing for me and heard their support.
c) My regret with this activity is that I did not find a way to complete my encounter with my own shadow. I was very aware, however, of how exhilerating and complete it was for many other people, and feel excited at the prospect of using it in my practicum with adolescents.
d) This activity was one of the most exciting I have ever taken part in. I have never given myself over to movement and music in such a free way, in my life–a truly treasured moment.
e) The dance between myself and my partner merged together. I was more aware of the shadows than the music. Sometimes the music was more inhibiting than calling out and I seemed to be working against it.
f) I would like to have danced alone in retrospect, in relation to my own shadow. It seems to require some guts to to look at yourself so directly.
g) Words from the dance: sorrow, covering, need, forgiveness, strength.

h) The most powerful for me was the oneness with the music.
i) I chose the people to play and directed them to the instruments that expressed what I had to say at that moment. It was a complete and total expression, with the music and my shadow as one.

EXPLANATION OF RITUAL

It was hoped that through the shadow and music, people would experience a symbolic or metaphoric death-rebirth, which they could identify with some specific situation or personality characteristic. This activity encouraged a group or person-to-person interchange.

The musical improvisation added a new dimension to the sessions. Whereas a recorded piece selected by the leader for its strong suggestion of death-rebirth, in a sense guides the results, the musical improvisation provides more freedom. The two key words in the instructions which suggested the death-rebirth direction were: 1) to the dancers, to find a state of "nothingness"; 2) to the instrumentalists, let your music "undulate". This new dimension is reflected in the comments, so that thematic content reflected greater variety. The musical improvisation also added a feeling of closeness between shadow dancers and instrumentalists, a feeling of respect, nurturing, sharing, understanding, mutually creating.

Several participants mentioned dealing with a split in their personalities. Some mentioned coming face to face with dark personality characteristics. which they feel resistant to change. In a sense, they engaged in a confrontation with some shadowy side. Again we see that something must be lost, or greatly transformed in order for new growth to occur.

Music and Movement

Music is movement and movement, music. Music suggests motion and through motion, growth and change. It is an action which comes to one, rather than a forcing. It is a sort of passive action. This is the motion between music and movement and man. This mythic motive was one of the first movements of man, not a frill, but a utilitarian gesture. How can we live if we do not dance? We dance the rain in times of drought. We dance pain and birth. We dance our brothers and sisters, the animals and trees and we are One. Life is motion. A newborn dances to the beat of his own heart and develops tiny muscles and touches the world. Every body and soul dances to the beat and breath of life, if we see and hear the dance. Watch the tree. The stillness comes to remind us of motion.

THE RITUAL

This session combined poetry and group movement with pre-recorded music. Group members participated in a warm-up in which they were encircled by a large material rope. They moved as a unit to some of the lighter, quicker Chopin Etudes. Then the lights were dimmed. This activity was used both as a warm-up and to provide a playful give and take task. Instructions for the main activity were as follows:

"Form a circle on the floor, head to the inside, each person in the curling leaf position, but holding hands with those on either side. Relax. Take even, normal breaths. Empty your mind of all thoughts. Find a feeling of stillness or nothingness. Imagine yourselves as one seed under the ground, if you wish. Only be aware of the warmth in the hands on either side. When the music begins, think of it as coming along the floor and into your body as nourishment. Let the music move you, only when you are ready and as slowly as you wish, in your own time. Keep your eyes closed and continue to hold hands with the people on either side''.

During the movement, people were encouraged to move in their own time, slowly, gradually. They moved as one unit, some ''growing'' slower, some more quickly. Chopin's Etude in A flat major was played three consecutive times. After the third time, a brief period of silence and stillness followed. Then participants were asked to come to a sitting position in the circle when they were ready. Each person was given paper and colored pen of their choice. The Etude was played again twice and people were asked to try to capture their feelings in poetic form–either in connection with previous movement or from the new listening.

Members were then asked to share their poems or any other feelings about the activity. The activity seemed incomplete for some; so participants were paired for more movement. The two criterion for pairing were:

1) People who shared a common feeling–They would have a time free from the restriction of group movement.
2) People who would share a balance–They would learn from each other through their different qualities.

They were asked to sit on the floor back to back, arms joined as a starting position. Again they moved to the A flat Chopin Etude.

A week later, the following responses were mentioned:

growing
flight and flying

rising and falling
calmness
lightness and solidarity
death-rebirth
relaxation
love
lifting and falling
crescendos
building
introspective
color in music
spaciousness allowed for high sensitivity
circles in repetition with a strong directional undercurrent
connected and alone at the same time
the quiet ending soothed me
contrast between high and low tones
flowing cycles and circles
soaring
like an ocean with waves coming in
swirling birth
tender feelings
seclusion and breaking away
fluid
flowing
gathering and expanding
gentle and assertive
lightness

Other extended responses were as follows:

a) I found sharing my poem harder than the rest of the activity.

b) My image was of fallopian tubes, leading to the nourishing hands, another way to get full.
c) I was aware of giving and taking.
d) It was difficult to bring myself out of the curled position, so I was glad to be holding hands. That contact stopped me from losing connection with other people. I was shaky and warm; introspective.
e) This activity was not introspective for me as others had been. It was a very meaningful and fulfilling to experience the sensation of balance and oneness with the music, my partner and myself. My body felt bigger, extended.
f) I like the idea of moving together, in a circle–the suggestion to keep in touch with others all the time restricted me. On the other hand, it is a life situation which occurs often.
g) The activity seemed disjointed–in sense of connection with each other and experience of music. My paired movement, on the other hand, was a very pleasurable experience. I think the writing enabled me to leave a past experience clearly.
h) The more I am successful in experiencing these sessions with a deeper, pre-verbal consciousness, the more difficult I find it is to call it up and back to the surface, linear thought. I feel contented for the most part to let the experience root deep and take its time coming up.

EXPLANATION OF RITUAL

Many people were able to experience a feeling of growing, whether in a sense of moving with the flow or struggling to maintain one's own identity under the pressure of group movement. Several mentioned the feeling of being split and having to make decisions about whether to assert one's own movements, or conform with the group movement.

Most experienced a sense of renewal. The theme of ability to accept nurturing or new life from others' activity was prevalent.

The embracing of paradox was a major theme–giving and taking, self and others, pain and joy. This theme was containe in Chopin's music as a result of his contrasting forms. A strong suggestion of rebirth came through the beginning positions of the participants–again in stillness, nothingness, each in a curling leaf or foetal position, holding hands in a circle. It was also the suggestion of a seed which grows from nothingness and absorbs the nutrients and growing elements of water, sun, music, warmth of the hands of others–all healing aspects of the environment.

Music and Poetry

Poetry is the music of the language. It sings, it rings, it plays with sound. It undulates and marches. It punctuates our thoughts more dramatically. It sends arrows through unnecessary semantics. It gives permission to use words in different ways. It contains rhythm, harmony, form, tension, resolution. In this way it complements music. The poet writes a song which becomes mythic legend, speaking for more than one.

THE RITUAL

The Music Therapy session which takes the least instruction is the combination of music and poetry. Even if the instructions do not say poetry, only stream of consciousness, poetry emerges. Instructions were "Let the music come into your ears and out through your pen in the form of words."

The following are patient poems to different pieces ~~of music~~.

Patient Poems To Pink Floyd's "Medley"

Stream of consciousness
Wending through open space
Leaf-like cascading over around
  through pebbles
Rocky surfaces submerged
Water surface mirrors green
  trees blue sky
Swirling in the reflection of God's country

Cast ashore, wind dried and tumbling over sweet
  smelling earth,
Inhaling the warm sun, dancing death to urban stress
Birth painfully to the spirits of well-being the
  spirit of self-destruction cries out for revenge.

But the natural self spirals deeper into itself, reborn
Cast adrift again to challenge the natural element on its
  own terms.
Not to win but to succumb successfully
Being one, strong in that natural partnership
Transcending self.

....and so they parted,
heading off to new, unexplored lands.

So the little blobs on the I are kind of mysterious
I am reminded of something that I did in a picture I
painted in grade XI.
13 dated little parts, different parts of me? actually
I like to see a unity amongst different parts based
upon conjunction

We are on another planet we are all friends and
still strangers to each other back on earth
Let's get to know each other in the time we
have left

The men in this projectile dies April 1, 1971
on the planet mars
They were in a projectile grave and floated up
towards the sun

Spaceship higher and higher
Fear of the unknown is terrifying
To die, to be reborn, who knows?

My time is long till I become reborn
But it just happened weeks ago didn't it
So why are you fighting love, trust and friendship with
words
Because I am being tortured by an unknown enemy
Hatred and revenge and words
The journey ends
But in the window comes air and out the window goes air

I would like to travel with all possible speed from the confining environs of Mother Earth, beyond the stellar horizon of our Sun. Look back disdainfully and sneer.

Then, dividing my own destiny, turn my back and only remember
the aquamarine, shrouded elyise. Casting relative time aside, ease further on the Phobos and there find my place of vantage.

After cutting a chink in the armour of Phobos, I would explore, with a sharpened eye; peer at the Crimson planet in her sleep. And watch the Blue Orb writhe and fade into indifference, consuming herself with envy and strife

Ding, ding, the bells call us to a mysterious land of enchantment.
Filled with fantastic images of flowers and ferns. The trail is long, over in the horizon one can see the sun slowly rising.
Clouds are travelling swiftly in the sky.
Onward alone I travel to the sea. Down by the shore I see the waves sparkling in the sun.
The water is inviting me to come in and relax in it. I remove my clothes and feel free to run along the sand bare foot.
At last I run into the cool water. I can see all sorts of fishes swimming and I swim with them.
I surface for air and refill my lungs. I dive deeper this time my curiosity is aroused. I want to swim farther away.

The current catches me and I am captured, left at the ocean's mercy.
I struggle to survive. I swim up to the surface but it is of no use. I want to scream but the water enters my mouth. In the distance I see one of man's creations. It is a submarine. I open the hatch and step inside. There are no human beings inside, only robots which are made to follow my requests. I ask them to take me on a journey to a distant land. They do not move.

Something is wrong, they don't care. They have not been used in two thousand years. I am the only human that exists since the nuclear war in 1990.
I exist only because God wills it. I lead a lonely life.
I repair the robots.
They can speak to me.
My life revolves around them.

Walking along the beach as the waves hit the shore
Lying in a meadow with all sorts of daisies
Walking alone downtown, feeling sad
Drinking coffee at a restaurant alone
Walking alone in a darkened forest
entering an enchanting forest
Watching the seagulls fly by
Walking by a stream
Listening to the crows caw
Such a lonely cry
Wind blowing through your hair
Strangers parading on by
Feeding the pigeons at pigeon square
Watching old men sitting on benches at pigeon square
Talking to strangers feeling lost and alone
In the early morning walking by the sea
Sitting alone on a log by the sea
Wandering across Burrard St. Bridge
Just walking downtown with no particular place to go
Walking down an endless highway
Watching the sailboats go by
Old man walking along by the sea

Metallic sounds of an elfin forge
Enchanted forests as a back-prop of Shadows & Sounds
The mood is broken by words that block out the peace
with their harshness of everyday definitions

The beat is stronger, a flowing & twirling promise of the unexpected
Where is it leading me can I safely give up my resistance?
Perhaps some harsh contrast will jolt me back too unexpectedly from my calm presence

Halloween visions of ghostly figures lured out of hiding by kind permission
Pale blue icy cold engulfs the figures in haze protecting the privacy of the moment
Clouds racing in from a wide open mood which casts shadows of forms that are lost in their passing

A stillness and calm. Kind resolution. A reward for chance-taking making the moment more significant through the experience.

A racing resistance to voices ē meaningless words. The wish to end with great resolution.

A magic garden
Birds pop
Delicate—then stretching to reach the warmth
Swaying thru light & dark, wet & dry
Denser swamp life—
  light moss above heavy wet sand
Romantic, misty touches of wind on grand oaks
Sand becoming denser—to heavy
Fingers light and tickled
As feet struggle with every step
I snap into a powerful rhythm of determination
Allowing me to walk on thru the muddy swamp glooy river.
Fear surrounds me in sounds and winds unfamiliar as I
plod into a continuous walking, rhythmic trance
Suddenly no longer heavy, but light & lost
a space walk through the swamp
As scary sounds embrace me piercing pain and no ground
to hold me
Lost with no direction. At least there is my friend the wind
Bats tease me
Such a strange form passing through them
An intense ray of sun bringing me a saviour in a heart beat—
the slowness forces me to appreciate the nourishment
It gradually begins to warm me, giving me strength
in my loneliest moment
Suddenly I am in the desert riding high & warm on a
stallion in a slow motion.
No longer the romantic but unfriendly, into celebration
of motion rhythm, light, strength
Rocking—inviting me to rise.

Patient Poems to Samuel Barber's "Adagio for Strings"

Man cold
Child warm
Superman? Is torn into clouds

The sun rises and brings death to darkness.

The warmth of the womb. Growth hot, vital strong.
There is an end. Slowly they become stronger moving
to meet themselves. Alone, independent, attached by
the pulse.

My mind wanders at wonders. A pearl, heavy with layered
coatings man and his life.

There is a vision that comforts a return to the womb, warm,
throbbing, enduring. The residual warmth cools slowly in
the head. The joining of lives, braids our collective soul.

Cold, empty blackened husk, its germ shrivelled and burnt.

The seed has its properties and message to grow
in a harsh world around a struggle so
difficult to live and easy to die
it continues to fight for it knows why.

It uses the elements in short supply
with no question or doubt but just to try
to survive and flourish day to day,
and flower and pass on the process this way

The seed is planted with loving care
The sun and the rain they are there
And the flowers that began the same
protectively circle and care
But the seed remembers the cold
of life before
and cries not to grow
Just to be in nothingness
no more pain no more ache
No more life
Gently the flowers give
their happiness away
so that the new seed
may forget the pain
and grow warm in their sun
the seed quivers
and begins again

As a seed under the ground I felt alone, darkness was all around and I had no friends. Gradually as I sprouted out of the ground I began to see how beautiful the world was. I saw the sun it was warm and good, I saw the trees swaying in the breeze, the clouds rolling in the sky all of nature was so friendly and it felt so good just to be there.

Patient poems to Oregon's "Become and Appear"

Lone wail as the sea rolls
imprisoned by winding shores
jungles echo the mysterious
rattle of snakes and dancing drums
lonely strange world encircling
me with a stronger and stronger beat
I want to run but every exit is covered
Snake charmers and strange frenzied
native surround and enclose my space.
The birds control the sky. Then I find
myself alone. I begin to explore, less frightened
now. The wind circles in a soft gesture and
makes me feel I belong. My spirit quickens
to foreign sights and sounds–the rattles lead
me deeper into the jungle–the drums beat a path
for me–I begin to dance the circle dance with the
natives and take their music into my soul–a
piercing whining sound arrests my attention–is it
a warning?–it passes and the music takes on a
more sinister tone. I race around for exits, but
once again the music soothes my fear and now I
rest.

The wind is roaring outside
The snake hisses
The pitter patter of little feet
I run outside and the sun
is shining brightly;
The tall trees, through them
I see the sun rays,
The daisies are strewn here & there.
I stop for breath and lay
down to rest on the green grass.

The tailor is cutting out fabric
for suits;
He stitches them together
His fingers are so nimble.

The sun riseth in the early
morning, its rays shining on
the little baby asleep in
a basket
He awakens and cries
for his mother who comes
out of the cottage to
pick him up

Dancing in the light
of twilight the young
girls made a pretty
picture; pirouettes
and soft tip toeing.

Space beyond time
Reaching
Forward, forever
Hollow moon
given
time and again
until
Nothing beyond.

Growing, upward
inward
outward
extending.
Never reaching
the forgotten
past.

Reaching
reaching
reaching
Extended time.
And again.

Nothing left
until tomorrow
the forever
beyond.

Dance left
until night
Given less
than move
too much
gone
and given.

Dark descends
moonless hollow
hollow moon
home for
many
forgotten few
given rest
to the rest
Until never.

Down the dark
hollow
dance out the
rhyme.

Knowing but not
given
Death imparts a
grace
G-race
God race
Given to
none.

Winnowing, winding, whirling on
and on thru the frozen air
blows the sailing wind. Unfurling
long billows of clouds that cover
the horizon like a carpet of
thick wavy mist.

Thumping and trumpeting wildly
thru the thin air comes the
triumphant trumpet as it shatters
the turbid air with voluptuous
trills.

Pounding, thumping as a massive
upheaval of earth ascends the
atmosphere making all below
cringe with disbelief.

Stomping, jumping running amid
the tiny rivulets.

Watching, waiting for a chance to
escape the dark night in its flight.

Running flirting flying thru the
dark mist–waiting watching
for the magic hour of repose
and rest.

Crashing symbols impart a feeling
of unique disbelief to the quiet
atmosphere.

A summer sky was overhead with cumulus clouds rolled into one end of it. There was intense heat from the sun and it bathed the world about in all its glory. There was an intense quietness in the scene around us. A ringed-pluner was circling high overhead giving out its plaintive cry of kill-dear, kill-dear. The rotten woods were standing tall and strong in the bright sunlight. A farmer was quietly working his land with a plow–the little boy was running barefoot along the road which the plow left on the hot earth. He could feel the cool-damp earth on his bare feet as he intently moved along the deep furrow. Looking along the wide field your eye moved to a clump of willow trees bending their branches close to the earth. A few blackbirds were flying quietly among the branches. In the distance the sound of a cow bawling could be heard. Among the lowest shrub a bush rabbit darted in search of his brothers and sisters. An eagle was sitting in a high poplar tree, his eyes searching for movement along the grassy ground. It was a perfect summer day. The smell of sweet-clover and honey-suckle permeated the air. Flies were flying among the grasses, restless, searching, pestering a small mouse that had run from the thicket to the open meadow. A farmer's boy disturbed the lazy summer silence with the sound of a pump handle squeaking up and down. A patch of yellow dandelions caught the long rays of the sun and shone up yellow and gold from the meadow's floor.

MUSIC IS THE SADNESS OF THE WORLD
MUSIC IS THE SADNESS OF THE SEED

HOW DOES ONE HAVE TO RELATE
TO EACH OTHER
WHEN YOU DON'T HAVE TO MEET

YET MUSIC IS BETTER THAN EVER
AND YET IT HAS TO MEET

REASONING IS BEYOND REASON
AND AS REASONING MEETS

SO THE MUSIC GOES ON
SAME AS THE WORLD GOES ON AND ON

Dawn over the sea
Whirling water
Birds wining
The sun burst–brilliant
dancing on the waves.

Tension lightens
Going around, spiralling
letting go relating
pink mountains
dancing skirts, multicoloured
stamping feet. Scarves curling
over arms. Smiling eyes.
lace mantuas–mysterious sensual

lonely shepherd in the hills
brown wrinkled skin–harsh
lines–rocky sheep jumping
ledges–lonely bird in the sky
whirling–sun beating.

Music and Color

If we can only see, music contains color. Therefore music suggests color. Paint is liquid and flows like music. It can be poured, brushed, layered, mixed. Color is vibration. It is what we sense about people–cool, electric, vibrant, textured, smooth. Color allows us to experiment by filling in the gaps in our personality. We try red. We softly approach blue. We pray purple. We see black which we have never cried until now. We laugh yellow. We place color in space. It has no time. We create and thus give new life to color.

THE RITUAL

One large roll of paper was stretched out for the group. Each person was provided with a brush, chosen by each for its texture and thickness. Rich tones of paint were provided–red, black, blue, yellow, green, brown, white and a couple of shades such as purple, amber, gold, etc. Combining paint and music, the group created a community painting.

Instructions were as follows: "This is a community painting. Let the music come in through your ears and out through your paint brush. Paint in your own space. If you wish, you may travel and paint in and around other people's space."

One piece used is Tchaikowsky's "Overture of 1812".

The group painting was then discussed and appreciated. As in the finest form of art therapy, the painters themselves assign meaning to color and form.

This can also be done with individuals in a solitary painting instead of a group painting. Patients are sometimes asked to improvise with musical instruments to the paintings. The paint provides another way for patients. Colors express the intensity of emotions, often diluted by words. In the community painting, secrets emerge, through the various interactions in paint. Anger, love, admiration, identification and other feelings are often shared through painting in and around another's work. This "first step" serves as the beginning of communication.

Music and Improvisation

There are hundreds of possibilities for musical improvisation. This technique represents a great deal of the work of Musical Therapists. Although the jazz or blues musician interprets musical improvisation as being a mutual agreement on some basic form and variations and interpretations of that form (e.g., 12-bar blues pattern, or a progression in G minor), musical improvisation for the Music Therapist usually follows a more spontaneous form. Development, interpretation, and variation of spontaneous music produced by the patient or client becomes the focus. Every note, every sound expresses something about that person. Although the music usually evolves into some form, the music in the beginning may be sustained in one or more tones, random and chaotic. These sounds are all accepted by the therapist as an expression of part of the human condition. They must be heard, accepted and shared. They often express the most basic and primitive side of our nature which becomes cluttered by more sophisticated music. If a child can find just the right instrument to express some secret side of his being, some lonely or painful or happy side, even though he may not speak, he expresses himself and therefore is free and grows, knowing he can communicate and share, if he so desires.

Many fine things have been written about Musical improvisation in Music Therapy in the works of Nordoff and Robbins, Mary Priestly and Juliette Alvin.

The following examples stress the approach of ritual within the Music Therapy Improvisation and recount two specific experiences. The first is a description of guidelines written at the Preschool for Special Children. Children with multiple handicaps were integrated with normal children of the same age in the Serendipity program at the Preschool for Special Children, University of British Columbia.

The second session was a teaching workshop with first-year Music Therapy students from Capilano College in Vancouver. In this one and a half hour session, Music Therapy was presented as ritual.

GUIDELINES FOR A CHILDREN'S SPONTANEOUS MUSIC WORKSHOP

Care should be taken to provide high quality tone from instruments in each family. The children should have great variety available to them for each family of instruments expresses different messages. In general, the following instruments should be included:

1) Drums and percussion–tambourines, woodblocks, maracas, etc.
2) Bells, gongs, sounding metals
3) Strings–guitars, harps, and string bass
4) Flutes, harmonicas, kazoos
5) Xylophones, piano, marimba

If funds are limited, it would be best to have one good instrument from each of the five categories.

The music room should be arranged with simplicity and respect. Children will learn to respect the instruments and their sounds if the therapist communicates a feeling of ceremony. They will then be able to use them as tools for meaningful expression. Instruments are arranged in a semi-circle with the gong and flutes in the center, drums and percussion to one side and the strings and other melodic instruments on the other side. Simple instruments which do not confuse the child with mechanical difficulties are best for the very young, but never "toy" instruments. Chanting, singing and dancing should be encouraged and space available for freedom of the dance.

ROLE OF THE ADULTS

Certainly everyone who is playing music is a person who has feelings, moods and ideas to communicate. This is an opportunity to "talk" about all these things without words. If the children feel that you are attending on this premise, they inevitably respond more openly and spontaneously. The musical experiences have much to offer in aiding development through the use of the child's own natural intervals, songs and chants. The old proverb states: "That which cannot be said can be sung, that which cannot be sung can be danced". It offers the child a chance to say "I'm angry" with a drum or "I'm happy" with a flute, "I'm strong" with a dance. Staff should be available for the sharing and expansion of feelings. One must be totally aware of the child, what he is trying to communicate, his changing moods, and respond accordingly, either by expressing that you know and understand the feelings by imitation, offering another alternative here and there, improvising on the theme offered by the child, and all the while using the child's body rhythms and chants as the base. There is also opportunity to make yourself known to the children, to offer direction when children are asking, but never to impose it within the music. Very often children will be creating an experience which they would rather handle themselves without staff direction. It is wise to stop before entering the music area, take notice of what is happening and decide whether your presence is required or not. The children will have a way of letting you know, but you must be aware of this possibility. Their play and experimentation with the sounds will have a different focus when an adult is present.

The workshops provide an opportunity for development in many areas. The children learn about expressive skills and communication. They also have a chance to develop motor skills. If they develop a special affinity for a certain instrument, the children will extend themselves beyond their limits to develop fine or gross motor skills.

Speech can be developed through flutes, harmonicas, kazoos, chanting and singing.

One of the most important considerations while playing spontaneous music is always to be ready to respond on any chants or sounds offered by the child. Often, though they may not have speech skills, these sounds are a beginning and even if they sound terrible to your ear, are very important to the child and need to be explored. Chant with her in imitation or add a bit of your own here and there to see if you might expand her chant to include more sounds, tones, intervals and build from there. Or just share hers for awhile. It may take away from the loneliness she experiences through physical limitations.

Music is a good place to learn ordering, patterning, sequencing. Children begin to expect a certain order, a particular progression in music, especially if it is something you have created together. Then it has a personal significance. The child feels a responsibility to develop the music if he has had a part in its formulation.

Another significant aspect of the spontaneous music workshop was the smooth and unthreatening structure offered for successful integration of all kinds of children. The different types of children with all their problems and joys could share and exchange emotions, sounds, dances, moods, and learn from each other whether they were developmentally delayed or functioning normally. They had many positive experiences with each other in music and therefore had more reason to strive to eliminate their limitations between each other. Through music they could share the core of themselves.

MUSIC IN THE HAIDA HOUSE

We met in the entrance hall of the Museum of Man, University of British Columbia. It was a slow night for the Museum. We seemed to be the only people there. With the absence of people, the spirits seemed more present. The totems spoke of timelessness, perhaps a greeting, an openness, a dignity. They certainly demanded respect and acknowledgment. The building itself was a curious combination of spaciousness and containment, past and present.

We gathered with our collection of musical instruments for the walk to the Haida House. It was dark and foggy with a horn calling from the surrounding misty bay. The walk through the forest was like a procession.

The Haida House itself was a small wooden structure, a miniature longhouse, similar to those used in many Native bands and tribes for ceremonial ritual. We had no fire in the center of the dirt floor. But small beams of light from overhead lamps suggested a bit of warmth and enough light to see each other and the instruments.

The Haida House was a surprise to most students, not the usual classroom portable. It was a little awesome, but allowed us to experience some of the sense of ritual as it was for the Native people.

We began in silence and seriousness. The students were asked to come up with a theme which represented a group belief. It had to be a theme agreed upon by the entire group for our ritual to have meaning. If this could be accomplished we would grow with and in the theme through our symbolic representations. We would leave with a sense of renewal and committment despite our individual differences. We would be community.

We spent 10 minutes in silence before someone gave the simple words which would constitute our theme for the evening: "We are all involved in a profession in which we both express and transcend". This seemed to ring true for all. It was a good theme, for it expressed one of the paradoxes of our work as Music Therapists.

We gathered in a circle around the imaginary fire. We each symbolically cupped the theme in our hands and placed it in the fire, returning slowly to the circle.

Then we held hands, closed our eyes, and began to chant. We hummed a few tones. Instructions were for one person to lead the chanting at a time, and the rest to complement. The leadership was to pass from one to another in random form. Whoever felt they were the leader would chant, we all would follow. The chant was to express our theme in individual ways.

Next the group selected "dancers", who were to dance the theme. The others would follow the dancers with musical improvisation. If the voice came, it could come from the dancers or instrument players. The dancers danced on the dirt floor and the instrumentalist played from the riser on the side. Flutes, drums, bells, shakers accompanied birds, panthers, trees, shamans, mothers.

Then the two groups switched.

We came together and chanted again as we had done in the beginning. On our final tune we sung the sound of the foghorn from the mist, waiting through the silence. We broke hands and retrieved our individual themes from the fire. They were richer

We took our instruments and left the Haida House. No one wished to speak. The quiet said it all.

The Journey

We see that each Music Therapy session is a journey. The idea of presenting therapy as ritual increases simplicity and complexity. The ritual should not weave a web of social value and convention, as do many rituals both present and past. It seeks only health and provides certain artistic forms which help participants travel to that health. We cannot write a script for another person's life, especially those at risk. We cannot demand what we might call a higher functioning level. We are all prisoners of our circumstances, whether we happen to be a terminally ill cancer patient, an autistic child, or a therapist who got up on the wrong side of the bed. We can only seek to balance and express and experience our common human characteristics. Through this sharing comes insight and regeneration. We can choose to accept suffering or fight disease if we remember the strength of human constants.

If we get disease out by externalizing and expressing, we are in a better position to fight an enemy.

The journey must be supported by a guide. The ritual forms must be strong and solid, and the basic beliefs only those common human processes which we observe in all of Nature, which surrounds us. Any behavior required by therapist from patient which extends beyond these primitive truths, risks the dangers of determinism.

As therapists, we guide the journey, guard and support the participants and aid them in identifying meaningful themes. From there the materials of the arts do the rest, to touch the human spirit and inspire her to create the art of the people.

Each therapist must be challenged to create meaningful ritual contexts which will be relevant to specific populations. There are degrees, levels, ways of presenting which will change and must be adapted. The above are merely ideas from which to spring. An important consideration is that often patients who cannot speak or who seem inarticulate are not able to give us the verbal feedback and reassurance we think we need in order to check ourselves. Related health professionals are sometimes equally incapable of serving as a check, since it is so difficult to describe musical events and their benefits with patients. In addition, the effects are often on the level of spiritual or intellectual insight and therefore not easily observed. We must tune ourselves to see and hear the response which is most difficult to observe–the inner response.

The important aspect of the mythical musical ritual in practice is that it does not allow us to separate and classify ourselves with disability nomenclature or job designation. For in its essence, it says that we are One. The forms and variations change but we all experience the human constants. We journey together into and through the music.

6 MUSIC THERAPY AS RITUAL

Although this approach to Music Therapy seems simple enough, a serious question arises when considering where and how to train these Music Therapy Ritualists.

It is clear that Music Therapy is an inter-disciplinary field. So the music therapist must be trained in many areas: Music, Psychology, Philosophy, Religious Studies, Art, Drama, Anthropology, Sociology, Ethnomusicology, etc. In addition to this academic training, the music therapist must understand on a personal level the workings of human nature, as much as possible.

These requirements seem to indicate a mature person with a Liberal Arts background and some life and work experience. These factors should be taken into consideration in screening applicants for training in Music Therapy.

In general, the music therapist must be the type of person who has respect for the following:

1) his/her own personality resources
2) resources of the client
3) processes inherent in music

4) processes inherent in structure offered
5) silence
6) time
7) space
8) history

In addition, the ritualist must develop confidence in self, others and the process of growth; flexibility and adaptability; empathy; strength; knowledge; humility; enthusiasm; humor and warmth; a sense of balance; good intention; and objectivity.

For the sake of liberation, the Music Therapist can be considered a Shaman. There are many references to the psychotherapist as Shaman. Jerome Frank says that the quiet, efficient attentions of today's physician do not, at first glance, seem to have any relation to the dramatic and emotion-filled rituals of the Shaman, But a closer examination indicates that the two have much in common.

1) Both derive their healing powers from their status and role within the sufferer's society.
2) Both are evokers of healing forces.
3) Both are mentors.
4) Both are role models.
5) Both mediate between the sufferer and their respective groups.

In general the task of both is to help the patient, whether African tribesman or North American stockholder, to mobilize his psychological and spiritual as well as bodily resources. Especially important for healing is the element of faith and trust placed in the therapist/shaman by the patient. Studies in the placebo effect have shown us how important faith really is. But in addition to the similarities between the psychotherapist and the shaman, the music therapist as a shaman is also an artist/music maker.

Areas shared between the shaman and the music therapist would be the following:

1) Both work with a magic phenomenon or art which is not totally understood.
2) Both work in professions having responsibility to oversee the health of the community, preventative and curative.
3) Both require the faith and trust of their communities in order to achieve results.
4) Both learn their skills and rely on their own judgment and intuition about when and where to apply them. They serve an apprenticeship and receive inspiration leading to insight about their work.
5) Both are dynamic personalities in that they are energetic and vigorous. Whether shy, gregarious, conservative or eccentric, they are still participating in activities initiated by themselves.
6) Both heal themselves by participating in their shamanistic art, either prior to or engaging in their vocation.
7) Both offer rituals and ceremonies intimately connected to myth and various art forms—music, dance, costume, color, etc.

The Artist

The Music Therapist is an artist by token of musical ability. But the value of the artistic nature of the musician within a context of ritual transcends technical and interpretive competence. As an artist, the ritualist has a certain way of perceiving the world which can be useful in healing and therapy.

The sensual perceptions of the artist allow the ritualist to guide the ceremonies and activities into profound representations of myth and life.

Since objectification or externalization is important in transformation, the Music Therapist must develop skills which encourage others to express: the Music Therapist externalizes and guides others to externalize feelings, thoughts, situational dilemmas, personality dynamics, into musical form. The music is immediate and constantly changing.

As an artist the Music Therapist is a resource combiner, experimenting and playing with alternatives. The artist draws, together all the resources and materials which will create a music therapy ritual. These resources would include everything which can be in the room at the time of the creation of the work of art: the personality qualities of all persons in the session, the environmental qualities of the space, the time of day, materials used (whether instruments, paints, record player or other), skills of all persons in the room, attitudes, cultural trends, history, beliefs, feelings, philosophies. In this situation the ritualist/artist becomes a facilitator.

One of the most essential qualities of the Music Therapist as artist is musical sensitivity. The ability to explore sound and silence freely and encourage ritual participants to do the same is essential. The artist should be able to hear and interpret unspoken moods, trained in both the form and flexibility of his instrument, able to combine his skills in unconventional ways, aware of the infinite variety of the language of music. She must use music as a meeting ground, a place in which to step outside conventional roles and patterns.

If the Music Therapist considers herself an artist, fulfilling her own creative instinct, and each music therapy session as a work of art, most probably clients will be inspired to follow suit. If this transfer is accomplished, the clients also become artists involved in creative processes. If allowed to be artists, it is possible that participants accomplish their own healing.

The Visionary

If the Music Therapist does assume the character and role of the ritualist/artist as mentioned above, it would imply the responsibility of vision as well. For the artist takes some initiative in the unfolding of the future through vision. This vision constitutes a plan, a scheme, a method of facilitating transformation of individuals and the culture itself. There are an infinite number of possibilities for visions–to see the visions of others is an important skill. Vision endows the Music Therapist with passion, conviction and moral responsibility, a sense of destiny and purpose, charismatic leadership qualities, an essential role in the evolution and improvement of culture and society. The presence of alternatives is a sign of vision. Vision has some unspeakable spiritual quality which is hard to define but can be heard within the music of the artist, a Ch'i (Chinese Vital Breath).

The visionary must be strong, yet subtle; clear yet undogmatic; the visionary must respect the visions of others.

The Initiate

The Music Therapist as Ritualist requires a particular type of training. This training is not necessarily available within the present academic institutions offering training in music therapy. Briefly, the Music Therapist as ritualist/artist/visionary must receive the following:

1) Experiences in all the various musical rituals presently available and encouragement to create new rituals dictated by the situational needs of each unique therapeutic environment. A trainee must personally experience the power of music and ritual.
2) Knowledge and skills in as many disciplines as possible, especially Music Therapy, Music, Philosophy, Psychology, Religious Studies, Anthropology, History, Creative Arts, etc. Equally important is a knowledge of one's own personal resources even before training begins.
3) Experiences in the field, i.e., in therapeutic environments, from the onset of training. This gives the trainee many levels of understanding, which can be guided by clients, other Music Therapists and professionals.

There must be a balance between the technical skills and information, and the character and personality who can accept and use the magic.

At the core of the musical, mythical framework as presented here is transformation. The ritualist must embrace transformation before and during rituals which present this process to others. If a prospective Music Therapist applicant has not embraced the process of change prior to training, this process is required during initiation/training. Again we are reminded of the shaman. There is a contrast between rigorous training and receipt of a diploma or purification and transformation.

The shaman and the yogi, the sorceress and the priestess, all derive their strength from an initiatory death and rebirth experience they must each undergo before they can truly be themselves. It is this transfigurative experience that endows them with their unique vision. In traditional society this experience is highly valued and the right to undergo it was

safeguarded religiously. But modern techno-historical society abolished the right to vision as well as the ritual for gaining it with a fearful self-righteous vengeance, thus ensuring its own fantastic rise to power but also sealing its own doom. In denying the validity of the vision and the vision-quest, modern society denied itself any rebirth short of apocalypse—an event its own shamans and visionary prophets, exiled to the sidelines, have continually foretold and prepared for.
(Josė Arguelles)[37]

The transformation of the trainee may be slight or extreme, but deep insight and understanding of the transformational process must occur, if she is to effectively employ the mythical, musical framework.

PART III

REFLEXIVE SYNTHESIS

As Arguelles speaks of our self-destructive urges toward apocalypse, Jerome Frank, in his book *Psychotherapy and the Human Predicament,* predicts the form of this eventual disaster as nuclear destruction and the cause, a type of social disease called technology. In Ivan Illich's words, we have heard this social disease called licentious technology. Because of this rampant technology, we are faced with the daily possibility of nuclear disaster, controlled by the emotions of political risings and fallings. While this cloud hangs over our daily lives, a fact which Frank sees in direct relation to the state of our mental health, we observe the simultaneous disappearance of fellow life on earth through the increasing disappearance of plant and animal species, including human species, all around us. The sick and distressed ones in our population are in direct relation to this situation. They are part of our essence. They are a reflection and intensification of our own collective condition.

There are many who consider the solutions to these problems can be formulated primarily on the drawing boards of nuclear physicists, in the halls of Congressional legislature, or in the laboratories of clinical psychologists. However, if we are to survive in a more total sense, we must also resurrect the most basic vehicles and rituals of human expression and creativity–the arts. Music and color, myth and ritual must resound from every home and we should see and hear the artists within. Some say we have already tossed away the vital threads of survival, that we are "on the way out". As long as we can still hear the heartbeat, as long as we can breathe, there is hope. The music reminds us.

The point is that something has gone wrong and what are the alternatives? What does the structure of magic have to offer a sick culture?

One clue is suggested by the word magic. We find magic where we do not have control of the elements of our lives. In this situation, perhaps we think we have control, by virture of our intellectual arrogance, when in fact we do not. We have created a dissociation of life from spirit.

The question for some is: Where have we gone wrong? The question used in the present document is: What have we left behind? In this situation of lack of balance, which elements of knowledge can we re-integrate into today's life in order to re-establish balance? The particular context used to address the question here is the therapeutic environment. But as stated earlier, these settings are only a reflection of the culture at large; and the people within those settings, reflections of the individuals outside.

What has been left behind by overuse of the medical model? The two predominant areas in this section are a lack of spiritual freedom, which might even be called a negation of spirituality, and a dearth of creativity, which from most artists' view is related to spiritual negation.

Here again we find the word spirit. Spirit implies

mystical, magical and religious experiences. Unfortunately the medical model has ignored this side of the nature of man. Some interpretations of psychoanalysis have gone one step further and labelled religion as neurosis. This has created unfortunate inadequacies in health care. The word religion, derived from the Latin re-, "back" and lingare, "to bind", means in its broadest sense "a binding back together". The opportunities for healing aspects of religion are obvious within this definition.

For the Navaho, medicine, religion and art are woven together in common purpose. Marvin Harris tells us that art, religion and magic all fulfill the same basic human needs. They break down the thin layer of ordinary appearance and go beyond to actual cosmic significance.

A more formal definition states that religion is the mixture of beliefs, attitudes, emotions, behavior, etc., constituting man's relationship with the powers or principles of the universe. This may or may not imply some function of deities. However, it assuredly does imply a seeking of ontological structures and frameworks which relate man to the broader universe. Frankl calls this man's search for meaning, and identifies this search as the essential ingredient in mental health or illness.

The primary aspect of creativity which emerges as a consideration in healing is acknowledgment and utilization of paradox, being able to accept and use mixed feelings or contradictory circumstances for growth and change.

The Death-Rebirth Myth and its infinite number of analogies in life, of course, is one example of such paradox. Effective ritual contexts for this myth have been left behind. Although there are some cultural rituals which, wittingly or unwittingly, employ this myth and other myths, there are not onough to reassure us or remind us of the basic ever-constant patterns of life, which Joseph Campbell calls the elementary forms or human constants. Within therapeutic settings, there are even less mythical rituals because of certain scientific, as opposed to spiritual, orientations. The anticipated product of ritual based on the Death-Rebirth Myth is transformation, growth and change.

If we are able to consider this process in ourselves as a reflection, and part of the world and universe around us, ontological questions are answered, and added strength and resources received. Similarly, if we view the environment and fellow life around us as a reflection of and part of ourselves, healing or prevention is reciprocal.

In order for this association to develop between man and nature, which surrounds him and is in him, connecting patterns must be appreciated. A noted Indian chief says: "All things are *connected*. Whatever befalls the earth befalls the sons of earth". [38]

Perhaps the metaphoric mind can see this vision more clearly than the logical mind.

Music is only one vehicle in this framework, but it does provide easy access because of the inherent healing processes. Unfortunately some of the processes inherent in music which can be used for healing have been ignored entirely because of strictly clinical orientation. In general these are:

1) Music contains magic.
2) Music is an aesthetic experience and therefore conducive to patterning.
3) Music can introduce and develop creative processes.

The Music Therapist as ritualist provides a context for the transformative experiences of mythical musical forms. In order to function in this role the music therapist must be not only clinician but also magician, artist as well as scientist and a visionary for the individual and the culture. She must understand and know the process of transformation personally in order to encourage others in this endeavor.

This text does not represent a purely systematic approach. Rather it represents a synthesized group of ideas which become alive within the use of the Mythical Musical Ritual. It does not provide answers to questions, but rather insights which lead us to wisdom. It is a framework to be suggested rather than imposed within certain sessions, within certain therapeutic environments when deemed appropriate by the music therapy ritualist. It strongly advises a pervasive change in present systems of therapy—a move to implement creative arts therapies. It suggests the feasibility of employing music as one of the vehicles for healing, in particular, the Death-Rebirth Myth. It also suggests certain qualifications necessary in initiation and transformation of Music Therapists creating ritual contexts for the mythical, musical structure. On a broader level it suggests an equal emphasis on art and science, a learning from, and incorporating of, certain traditional ideas within our present situation, a binding back to nature.

It reminds us that we are not separate from the suffering peoples. We relate to each other through that which we share as humans. We come together through soul. Symbol, ritual, music and myth are a celebration of this unity as well as a vehicle for practical growth. Through music, color, form, shape, texture, touch, we perceive this unification. We work on survival and improvement. This is the healing power of the arts.

Through the eyes of Angel Babies on backwards, through the anger of prisoners, through the silence of autism, through the music of the therapist, we see this vision and experience soul, sharing the same artery of life. Music and myth are suggested as only one of the means through which to return to these considerations. Sufi Inayat Khan says:

> *Music is the harmony of the universe in microcosm; for this harmony is life itself, and in man, who is himself a microcosm of the universe.*[39]

The Mythic Artery recalls our childlike wisdom, the beginers mind and heart. It re-establishes our connections to the heritage of human events. It binds us to Nature. It gives us nurturing and renewal of the liquid qualities of the arts. It refreshes our soul. The music heals, if we will only hear.

Summer Solstice

Santa Barbara, California

1980

The drums of Shiva,
The bells of Islam–
No Marine bands approach
This celebration of Solstice.
Bangles, costumes, colors of the East,
South America, the Native Indian
Music of the peoples of Black, Red and Yellow
March on this day
Through the sons and daughters of the sixties
In Western sun.

Twenty years later they remind us
Of the heartbeat, the breath...
What have we left behind?

There is no death
For this culture
Who hears the heartbeat
Across many miles.

Where is the myth in our own music?
Hear the beat
It is the same drum.
The cosmic tree
Stretches across the Earth
As does the wind
Who knows no East or West.
We assign names to space
But the Earth has one core
which is always at the center.

Hear the mythic music which binds and heals
For sons and daughters
Of East and West.

Carolyn Bereznak Kenny

FOOTNOTES

(For complete references, please see the Bibliography.)

1. Rogers, p. 348
2. Ibid., p. 348
3. Freud, p. 327
4. Maduro, from Gordon, p. 135
5. Sinnott, p. 107
6. Task Panel, p. 1961
7. Ibid., p. 1942
8. Eiseley, *The Night Country*, p. 130
9. Szaz, p. 69
10. Bateson, p. 40
11. Strupp, p. 7
12. Task Panel, p. 1978
13. Frankl, p. 110
14. Hillman, p. 3
15. Illich, p. 35
16. Arguelles, p. 290
17. Larsen, p. 3
18. Whitmont, p. 18
19. Levi-Strauss, p. 193
20. Moerman, p. 60
21. Rumi, from Schimmel, p. 7
22. Gurdjieff, from Schimmel, p. 7
23. Steindl-Rast, p. 22
24. Eliade, p. 135
25. Keleman, p. 23
26. Eiseley, *The Star Thrower*, p. 118
27. Chief Sealth, speech reprinted in Greenpeace Chronicles
28. Sandner, p. 273
29. Bateson, p. 127
30. Sinnott, p. 113
31. Hindemith, p. 257
32. Khan, p. 3
33. Levi-Strauss, from Hopkins, p. 250
34. McLaughlin, p. 87
35. Khan, p. 2
36. Kapferer, p. 3
37. Arguelles, p. 288
38. Chief Sealth, op. cit.
39. Khan, p. 97

Apel, William. *Harvard Dictionary of music*, Cambridge, Mass.: The Belkap Press of Harvard University Press, 1969.

Arguelles, Josè. *The Transformative Vision*, Shambhalla, Berkeley and London, 1975.

Arieti, Silvano. *Creativity: The Magic Synthesis*, New York: Basic Books, Inc., 1976.

Assagioli, Robert. "Psychosynthesis: A Technique for the use of Intuition", *Pyschosynthesis: A Manual of Principles and Techniques*, Hobbs, Dorman & Company, 1971. In Ornstein ed., *The Nature of Human Consciousness*.

Bateson, Gregory. *Mind and Nature*, New York: E. P. Dutton, 1979.

Beeker, Ernest. *The Denial of Death*, New York: The Free Press, 1973.

Bogan, Joseph. "The Other Side of the Brain: An Appositional Mind", Bulletin of the L.A. Neurological Societies, 34, No. 3. In Ornstein ed., *The Nature of Human Consciousness*.

Bony, Helen & Savary, Louis. *Music and Your Mind,* New York: Harper and Row, 1973.

Camp, John. *Magic, Myth & Medicine,* New York: Taplinger Publishing Company, 1974.

Campbell, Joseph. *Hero of a Thousand Faces,*New York: Pantheon Books, 1949.

Campbell, Joseph. *Myths to Live By,* New York: The Viking Press, 1972.

Campbell, Joseph. *The Masks of the Gods: Primitive Mythology,* New York, Viking Press, 1959.

Chaplin, J.P. *Dictionary of Psychology,* New York: Dell Publishing Company, 1968.

Chilton-Pierce, Joseph. *The Magical Child,* New York: E. P. Dutton, 1977

Critchley, Macdonald & Henson, R.A. *Music and the Brain,* London: William Heinemann Medical Books, Ltd., 1977.

Cross, Milton & Ewen, David. *The Milton Cross New Encyclopedia of the Great Composers and their Music,* Garden City, New York: Doubleday & Co., 1953.

d'Aquili, Eugene G., Laughlin, Charles D., McManus, John. *The Spectrum of Ritual: A Biogenetic Structural Analysis,* New York: Columbia University Press, 1979.

Deikman, Arthur J. ''Bimodel Consciousness'', *Archives of Psychology,* 25, December, 1971, 481-489. In, Ornstein ed., *The Nature of Human Consciousness.*

Dimmitt Church, Cornelia. "Myth and History as Complementary Modes of Consciousness", In *Myth and the Crisis of Historical Consciousness,* eds., Lee W. Gibbs & W. Taylor Stevenson, Missoula, Montana: Scholars Press, 1975.

Dooling, D.M. "The Dangerous Passage", *Parabola,* Vol. 4, Fall 1976.

Eiseley, Loren. *Night Country,* New York: Chas. Schribner's Sons, 1971.

Eiseley, Loren. *The Star Thrower,* New York: Times Books, 1978.

Eliade, Mircea. *The Myth of the Eternal Return,* New Jersey: Princeton University Press, 1954.

Eliade, Mircea. *Rites & Symbols of Initiation,* New York: Harper & Row Publishers, 1958.

Fleshman, Bob, and Fryrear, Jerry. *The Arts in Therapy,* Chicago: Nelson-Hall, 1981.

Frankl, Viktor E. *Man's Search for Meaning,* Boston, Beacon Press, 1959.

Frank, Jerome D. *Psychotherapy and the Human Predicament,* New York: Shocken Books, 1978.

Freud, Sigmund. *A General Introduction to Psychoanalysis,* New York: Boni and Liver right, 1920. In Pickering, *The Creative Malady,* New York: Dell Publishing, 1974.

Garfield, S. & Bergin, A.E. *Handbook of Psychotherapy & Behavior Change*, 2nd ed. Toronto: Wiley & Sons, 1978.

Gaston, Thayer E., ed. *Music in Therapy*, New York: Macmillan, 1968.

Gordon, Rosemary. *Dying and Creating a Search for Meaning*, London: The Society of Analytical Psychology, Ltd., 1978.

Greenpeace Chronicles, Vancouver, British Columbia, November, 1979.

Grinder, John & Bandler, Richard. *The Structure of Magic*, Vol. 1 & 2, Palo Alto, California: Science and Behavior Books, 1976.

Halpern, S. *Tuning the Human Instrument*, Palo Alto, California: Spectrum Research Institute, 1978.

Hamel, Peter Michael. *Through Music to the Self*, Wiltshire: Compton Press, 1976.

Harris, Marvin. *Culture, People, Nature*, New York: Thomas Cromwell, 1971.

Helmholtz, H.L.F. *On Sensations of Tone*, 1862 Trans. Ellis, 4th ed. London: Langmans, Green & O. Ltd., 1912.

Hillman, James. *Re-visioning Psychology*, New York, London: Harper Colophon Books, 1975.

Hindemith, Paul. *A Composer's World*, Boston: Harvard Press, 1969.

Hopkins, Pandora. "The Homology of Music & Myth: Views of Levi-Strauss on Musical Structure", *Ethnomusicology*, Vol. 21: 2 May 1977, pp. 247-261.

Illich, Ivan. *Medical Nemesis*, Toronto: Bantam Books, 1976.

Jilek, Wolfgang. *Psychohygenic & Therapeutic Aspects of The Salish Guardian Spirit Ceremonial*, M.A. Thesis, University of British Columbia, 1972.

Johnston, William. *Silent Music*, New York, London: Harper & Row Publishers, 1974.

Jung, Carl. *Symbols of Transformation*, Princeton, New Jersey: Princeton University Press, 1956.

Kapferer, Bruce. "Mind, Self, & Other in Demonic Illness: the Negative & Reconstruction of Self". *American Ethologist*, Vol. 6 #1, February, 1979.

Kapferer, Bruce. "Ritual Process and the Transformation of the Context", *Social Analysis* - No. 1, Adelaide, S.A.: University of Adelaide, February, 1979.

Keleman, Stanley. *Living Your Dying*, New York: Random House Press, 1974.

Keyes, Laurel Elizabeth. *Toning: the Creative Power of the Voice*, Marina Del Rey, California: Devorss & Co. Publishers, 1973.

Khan, Inayat. *Music*, Lahore, Pakistan: Sh. Muhammad Ashraf, 1971.

Kiev, Ari. *Magic, Faith and Healing*, London: The Free Press, 1904.

Koestler, Arthur. *The Act of Creation,* New York: The MacMillan Co., 1964.

Langer, Susanne K. *Form & Freedom*, New York: Chas. Scribners Sons, 1953.

Larsen, Stephen. *The Shaman's Doorway,* New York, London: Harper & Row Publishers, 1976.

Leonard, George. *The Silent Pulse,* New York: E. P. Dutton, 1978.

Levi-Strauss, Claude. *Structural Anthropology,* Garden City, New York: Doubleday Books, 1967.

Linklater, Kristin. *Freeing the Natural Voice,* New York: Drama Book Specialist Publishers, 1976.

Luce, Gay. "Biological Rhythms", *Biological Rhythms in Psychiatry & Medicine,* National Institute of Mental Health, 1970. In Ornstein ed., *The Nature of Human Consciousness.*

Lundin, Robert W. *An Objective Psychology of Music,* New York: The Ronald Press Co., 1967.

Malinowski, Bronislaw. *Magic, Science & Religion,* Garden City, New York: Doubleday Books, 1948.

May Rollo. *The Courage to Create,* New York: W.W. Norton & Co. Inc., 1975.

McLaughlin, Terence. *Music and Communication,* London: Faber & Faber, 1970.

Mead, Margaret. *Ruth Benedict,* New York, London: Columbia University Press.

Meyer, Leonard B. *Emotion & Meaning in Music,* Chicago, London: University of Chicago Press, 1956.

Meyer, Leonard B. *Explaining Music,* Chicago, London: University of Chicago Press, 1973.

Moerman, Daniel E. "Anthropology of Symbolic Healing", *Current Anthropology,* Vol. 2p, HI, March 1979, p.p. 59-80.

Neher, Andrew. "A Physiological Explanation of Unusual Behavior in Ceremonies Involving Drums" in *Human Biology,* Vol. 34, #2, p.p. 151-161.

Neumann, Erich. *Art and the Creative Unconsciousness,* Princeton, New Jersey: Princeton University Press, 1959.

Ornstein, Robert E. *The Nature of Human Consciousness,* San Francisco: W.H. Freeman & Co., 1973.

Ornstein, Robert E. *The Psychology of Consciousness,* San Francisco: W.H. Freeman & Co., 1972.

Parabola, "The Nature of Death", Vol. 2 #1, Winter 1977.

Pickering, George. *The Creative Malady,* New York: Dell Publishing Co., 1974.

Reik, Theodor. The Haunting Melody, New York: Farra, Strauss, Young, 1953.

Revesz, G. *Introduction to the Psychology of Music,* University of Oklahoma, Norman, 1954.

Rogers, C.R. "Towards a Theory of Creativity" (1954), ed. Vernon, P.E., *Creativity,* Penguin Books, Middle Sex, 1970.

Rosenbook, David. *Biofeedback and the Arts,* Vancouver, Aesthetic Research Institute of Canada, 1976.

Rothenberg, Albert. "Creative Contradictions", *Psychology Today,* Vol. 13, June, 1969.

Task Panel Reports Submitted to the Presidents Commission on Mental Health, Vol. IV, 1978.

Samples, Bob. *The Metaphoric Mind,* Don Mills, Ontario: Addison-Wesley Publishing Co., 1976.

Sandner, Donald. *Navaho Symbols of Healing,* New York, London, Harecourt Brace Jovanovich, 1978.

Schafer, Murray A. *The Tuning of the World,* Toronto: McClelland & Stewart, 1977.

Schimmel, Annemarie. "Die & Become", *Parabola,* Vol. 3, #2, May, 1978.

Seashore, C.E. *Psychology of Music,* New York: McGraw Hill, 1938.

Shapiro, A.K. "Factors contributing to the placebo effect, their implications for psychotherapy", *American Journal of Psychotherapy,* 18: 73-88, 1964.

Sinnott, E.W. "The Creativeness of Life", *Creativity*, ed. Vernon, P.E. Middlesex: Penguin Books, 1970.

Solomon, Philip & Patch, Vernon D. *Handbook of Psychiatry*, Los Altos, California: Lange Medical Publications, 1974.

Sontag, Susan. *Illness as Metaphor*, New York: Farrar, Straus & Giroux, 1978.

Strupp, Hadley, Gomez, Schwartz. *Psychotherapy for Better or Worse...an Analysis of Negative Effects*, New York: Jason Aronson, 1977.

Steindl-Rast, Brother David. "Learning to Die", *Parabola*, Vol. II, #1, Winter, 1977.

Stent, Gunther S. "Limits to the Scientific Understanding of Man", *Science*, 187: 1052-57, 1975.

Storr, Anthony. *The Dynamics of Creation*, London: Secker and Warburg, 1972, In, Pickering, G., *The Creative Malady*.

Sullivan, J.W.N. *Beethoven, His Spiritual Development*, New York: Vintage Books, 1960.

Sykes, Gerald. Alienation, *The Cultural Climate of our Time*, New York: George Braziller, 1964.

Szasz, Thomas S., M.D. *The Myth of Mental Illness*, New York: Harper & Row Publishers, 1974.

Szasz, Thomas S., M.D. *The Sacred Symbol of Psychiatry*, New York: Basic Books Inc., 1976.

Weckman, George. "Believing Myth as Myth", *Myth the Crisis of Historical Consciousness*, ed. Lee W Gibbs & W. Taylor Stevenson, Missoula, Mont.: U S.A. Printing Dept., 1975.

Van Genner, Arnold. *The Rites of Passage,* Chicago: Chicago University Press, 1960.

Vernon, P.E *Creativity,* Middlesex, England: Penguin Books, 1970.

Whitmont, Edward C. *The Symbolic Quest,* Princeton: Princeton University Press, 1969.

Whorf, Benjamin Lee. "Language, Mind, Reality", J.B Carroll, ed. *Language, Thought & Reality: Selected* Writings of Benjamin Lee Whorf, Cambridge, Mass.: The MIT Press, 1956. In, Ornstein ed., *The Nature of Human Consciousness.*

Willems, Edgar. "Introduction a la therapio musicale", in Schweizerischa Muzikzeitung, Vol. 3, 1963.